Winners and
LOSERS

ANNE SCHRAFF

SADDLEBACK
EDUCATIONAL PUBLISHING

2/13

PA

URBAN UNDERGROUND ®

SADDLEBACK
EDUCATIONAL PUBLISHING
www.sdlback.com

© 2012 by Saddleback Educational Publishing

ISBN-13: 978-1-61651-962-9
ISBN-10: 1-61651-962-2
eBook: 978-1-61247-644-5

Printed in Guangzhou, China
0512/CA21200822

16 15 14 13 12   1 2 3 4 5

CHAPTER ONE

Who do you think you are, Sandoval?" came a voice as sharp as a razor. Ernesto Sandoval was heading for his first class at Cesar Chavez High School. It was his first morning as a senior. It was his first morning as senior class president.

Rod Garcia was a tall, thickly built senior who thought he should have been class president at Chavez. Ever since he was a freshman at Chavez, Rod Garcia joined the right clubs and took part in the most important activities. His one goal was to be senior class president.

But Ernesto, a newcomer, took it away from him. Ernesto had been a total outsider when he arrived from Los Angeles last year.

Although his parents were from this *barrio*, Ernesto had grown up in Los Angeles. That was all he knew. Luis Sandoval, Ernesto's father, had taught history at a Los Angeles high school. Then the school downsized, and he lost his job. When he was offered a job teaching American history at Cesar Chavez High School, he jumped at it. Ernesto's parents were coming home to where they lived as children and young adults. To Ernesto, though, the move was strange and scary.

Ernesto had come to Chavez last year as a junior. He was scared, insecure, a loner who wasn't sure if he'd ever fit in. Those first few days, Ernesto made just one friend. A guy named Abel Ruiz took pity on the lonely outsider standing in the shadows. If not for Abel, Ernesto thought he would not have made it through the year. He then made other friends quickly, and pretty soon he was feeling at home. Later in his junior year, Ernesto's friends urged him to run for senior class president. He didn't think he'd win. But now that he had, Ernesto was determined to be the best senior class president ever. He was going to make a difference for all the kids.

"Uh, hi, Rod," Ernesto greeted. Ernesto was never close to Rod, but last year they used to say "Hi" to one another when they passed on campus. Ernesto didn't quite know how to deal with Rod now.

"You think you're pretty hot stuff, don't you, Sandoval?" Rod snarled. The depths of his hostility stunned Ernesto. He knew the guy was disappointed that he didn't win, but he never thought Garcia was this bitter.

"No, Rod . . . I, uh . . . don't think that," Ernesto stammered. "I'm just a guy who loves our school and wants to help the seniors."

"You came out of nowhere, you little punk!" Garcia stormed. "Only talent you got is undermining other people. I was going to be a great senior class president. Everybody said I deserved it and I'd get it. You,

3

a nobody, you come out of nowhere. You hang with dirty homies and taggers. You took it away from me." The hatred spewed from Garcia like lava from a volcano.

"Hey," Ernesto finally found the courage to say, "I entered the election fair and square, man. The kids could've voted for anybody. I didn't do anything wrong. The kids voted for me, okay? And I don't hang out with gangbangers, dude."

Rod Garcia laughed. "Every little creep at this school with a rap sheet is your bro. Dom Reynosa and Carlos Negrete have tagged every wall in the *barrio,* and you're in solid with them. That thug, Paul Morales, he hangs with hardcore criminals, and you're his homie."

"Look, those are good guys who've had problems," Ernesto came back. "You should have such good friends. They're trying to—"

"Yeah, right," Garcia interrupted. "Shaved heads and tattoos and hoodies. Morales has a rattlesnake tattooed on his

4

hand. I remember him when he went to Chavez. He was a snake. Those are your kind, Sandoval. I bet most of your uncles and cousins up in LA are in prison or haven't been caught yet. And now you're our senior class president," Rod Garcia hissed. "Go figure!"

"Look, man, I don't deserve this," Ernesto countered, a little shakily. His hand trembled. He'd never been the subject of such a barrage of hatred. He'd never seen it coming. He didn't hang with Rod Garcia's friends. They were from a better neighborhood than where Ernesto and his friends lived. True, Ernesto felt more at home with his friends, but he tried to treat everybody with friendliness.

"Another thing, man," Rod continued. "You've ruined the Chavez Cougars. We had a football team headed for the division championships. Then you slithered down from LA and took the heart right out of the team. Clay Aguirre was our star. But you moved in on his chick, Naomi Martinez, and took her away. That drove Clay down and ruined his game, and you know it. Our team tanked last year, thanks to you. I'm telling you, man, you're like poison gas around here."

At that point, Ernesto felt a lot like that first day he walked onto the campus of Chavez High. He felt like everybody was against him. He felt like some alien who just stepped off a spaceship, surrounded by angry Earthlings. Ernesto was shocked that Garcia could drain away all his self-confidence so easily. He felt vulnerable and sick. He stared at Garcia for a moment and then said the first thing that came to mind.

"Right now, I don't know who's the bigger idiot. You or Aguirre. . . . I gotta get to AP History," Ernesto mumbled, turning away.

Rod Garcia crowed, "You're gonna have Quino Bustos, man. He's the toughest teacher in the school. I'm in the class too. He'll see right through you, Sandoval.

He'll see you're a phony, a big mouth with nothing to back it up. I hope he flunks you, man. I hope you flunk all your classes." With that Garcia wheeled and stalked off.

Ernesto felt as though he'd just been ambushed. He thought this was how his dad felt in Iraq a few years ago when his unit hit an IED at a place they thought was secure. Dad ended up almost losing an eye. Now he carried a scar on his right cheek from the close call. Ernesto had no scar from Garcia's attack, but he was shaken.

On his way to class, Ernesto ran into Abel Ruiz, his best friend. "Oh man, Abel, I just walked into a buzz saw," Ernesto groaned, his voice uneven.

"What went down, dude?" Abel asked.

"Rod Garcia," Ernesto answered. "He's really ticked that I won senior class president. He unloaded on me just now like I'd killed his brother or something. I don't know him that good. Is he some kind of a psycho or what?"

"He's hot tempered," Abel explained. "He wants what he wants. You don't cross him. He's always got what he wanted. His father is a big financial advisor who makes good money. His mother teaches at the community college. Only kid. He's the only student at Chavez driving a BMW. I guess you taking senior class president away from him is the first big downer in his life."

"Man, I feel like I was mauled. The guy's a grizzly," Ernesto said.

"Probably his old man is giving him a hard time about losing," Abel suggested. "He once said his father liked to say, 'Only losers lose.' He'll get over it."

"Yeah? I wonder," Ernesto responded.

Ernesto walked on alone toward his AP History class. It was a tough class. He knew that going in. But he planned to go to law school, and he thought he better get used to tough classes. His uncle Arturo, a local *abogado*, had told him how hard law school was. But Ernesto had his heart set on it.

Ernesto was disappointed in himself for letting Garcia get to him so bad. He should have given as good as he got. Instead, he reverted to being that scared junior who hit the campus last year. At the time, Cesar Chavez High was sort of a big block of ice that he couldn't penetrate. Ernesto was much skinnier then and a bit shorter. Now he was six foot two and really built. He lifted weights, ran, and worked out almost every day. He was ripped. Even his little sisters, nine-year-old Katalina and seven-year-old Juanita, said he looked good. Ernesto now weighed more than his father, who was fairly well built himself. Still, he felt like the skinny little rabbit of last year after the barrage of hatred from a red-faced Rod Garcia.

Mr. Joaquin "Quino" Bustos was already at his desk when Ernesto entered the AP History classroom. There were about twelve students, including Rod Garcia, who was already seated in front. Garcia was having a cordial conversation with Mr. Bustos about their differing opinions on Thomas Jefferson and Alexander Hamilton. They sounded like colleagues, not student and teacher.

Chills went up Ernesto's spine as he headed for the middle of the classroom. He didn't recognize anybody in the class. He saw several scholarly looking boys and four serious-faced girls. For a panic-stricken moment, Ernesto considered bolting out of the room and dropping this course, if he could, in exchange for something less intimidating.

Ernesto got a grip on himself and sat down. He answered in a calm voice when Mr. Bustos called his name in the roll.

"Well," Mr. Bustos began, "how do we understand the birth of the American nation? First, we must grasp the mighty conflict that went on between the Federalists led by Alexander Hamilton and the Jeffersonians. Can someone comment on the conflict?"

Rod Garcia's hand shot up. "I spent a lot of time this past summer studying this,"

Garcia announced. "I read some books, went on the Internet, and got into original sources. I ended up very partial to Jefferson's vision."

"Excellent!" Mr. Bustos declared. "I hope that all of you are as well prepared through copious reading. Who wishes to speak on behalf of the Federalists?"

Ernesto wanted only to remain silent and, if possible, become invisible to Mr. Bustos's piercing black eyes. With his wild, unruly hair and shining eyes, Bustos looked a bit like a madman. But, in a reckless moment, Ernesto raised his hand.

"Yes, uh . . . Ernesto?" Mr. Bustos had had to check his roster for Ernesto's name. Now his eyes locked on Ernesto like a laser beam.

"I believe Alexander Hamilton saw more clearly into the future than Jefferson did," Ernesto proposed. He was grateful for the arguments he'd had with his father over the past summer on these issues. Ernesto's father was an excellent history teacher.

11

"Hamilton saw the end of the agrarian society while Jefferson clung to that vision."

"Ahhh, indeed so," Mr. Bustos agreed, pleased.

Ernesto's legs felt weak, but he figured he'd made a good first impression. He was a good student. There was no doubt of that. He didn't mind working hard and amassing tons of research. He faced a lot of writing in this class, and he wasn't afraid of that. Passing this course would give Ernesto a leg up on college. Advanced placement classes offered college credit.

The rest of the morning went well for Ernesto. He liked his English teacher, an amusing middle-aged lady named Grace Lauer. He also liked his biology teacher, gray-haired Sam Ardith. He was relieved when he headed for lunch with his friends—Abel, Naomi Martinez, Carmen Ibarra, and a few others. The knots had loosened in his stomach, and he was slowly getting over Garcia's attack on him this morning.

Ernesto bought two tacos and a carton of orange juice, and he brought them to the shady spot where the seniors ate. He told everybody about his encounter with Rod Garcia.

Carmen Ibarra—whose father was City Councilman Emilio Zapata Ibarra—sneered at the sound of Garcia's name. "He's such a jerk," she declared. "He looks down on everybody. He's almost a bigot. I mean, he's Hispanic like we are, but he sees us in two separate groups. There's the ones with money like his family. Then there's the rest of us. He thinks all the kids from Oriole and Wren and the bird streets are scum. The other day, he was griping about how everybody speaks different languages in town. He's sayin' it's un-American or something. He doesn't like to hear the Middle East storekeepers."

She stabbed a spoon into her yogurt as if she was sticking a pin in Rod Garcia. "I told that jerk that a hundred years ago in American cities, people spoke German and Yiddish, Polish, Greek, Italian—you name it. Now some people speak Arabic, Vietnamese, and Spanish. So what? That's what makes our country so great. We get the best people from all over the world. They come here and enrich us, like lots of great spices make a fabulous stew."

Carmen pitched a spoonful of yogurt into her mouth and munched on it. In a second, she was ready to speak again. "But Rod wasn't buying that. 'You speak English right now or go back to where you come from,' he says. Ugh! He's a bigoted moron." She stabbed her yogurt again and shoveled another spoonful into her mouth.

Ernesto recalled what Rod had said about Paul Morales, Carmen's boyfriend. He called him a thug and a snake. But Ernesto didn't want to make Carmen feel bad, so he didn't repeat the slurs. But Carmen was smart. She detected a strange look in Ernesto's face. She looked directly at him and said, "I bet Rod was dissing Paul and some of the other guys too, huh?"

"Yeah," Ernesto admitted. "He said I hang out with homies and taggers. He said most of my relatives up in LA are probably in prison."

"What a total creep!" Carmen wailed, now peeling her orange vigorously, taking out her anger on the orange.

"Yeah, he even accused me of ruining the Chavez football team because I'm dating you, Naomi," Ernesto said, turning to the beautiful girl with violet eyes. He loved Naomi more than his own life. "He said when Clay lost you, he wasn't a good football player anymore. It wrecked the Cougars. They went into the tank."

Naomi laughed. "Clay got kicked off the football team because he wouldn't study and his grades got too low." Once Naomi had loved Clay Aguirre. That was the truth. He treated her badly, though, for a long time. He was always insulting her and once told her how stupid she was when she forgot to turn in a paper she was doing for him. Then he went too far. He

15

slapped Naomi so hard across the face that she was badly bruised. That was the end of the relationship. Naomi would not take that from anybody, not even from someone she loved. It took her a while to completely lose her feeling for him, but it finally happened.

"Just ignore Garcia," Abel advised as he finished his soda. "He'll get tired of getting on your case, Ernie. You got plenty of friends, dude. After all, we elected you our senior class president, didn't we?"

Everybody laughed then and headed for afternoon classes.

After his first full day at Chavez High, Ernesto jogged home. Sometimes Ernesto drove his old white Volvo to and from school. But on most days, especially when the weather was nice, he jogged home. Sometimes he even took out his old skateboard and went flying down the street like a middle schooler. He remembered being thirteen and fourteen in Los Angeles, without a care in the world.

Chavez High School sat on Washington Street. Ernesto had to jog just a few blocks and turn on Tremayne. His street, Wren, was the third off Tremayne. All the streets were named for birds because the developer liked birds. Naomi Martinez lived on Bluebird Street and Carmen on Nuthatch. Guys like Rod Garcia and Clay Aguirre lived someplace else, on nicer streets with bigger houses.

Ernesto liked his neighborhood, though. He thought it was one of the friendliest in the *barrio*. The people didn't have a lot of money, but they kept up their houses. Geraniums were very popular because they were easy to share and grow. Just cut off a stem with a node on it, stick it in the ground, and off it went. Red, pink, and white geraniums grew everywhere on Wren Street.

As Ernesto jogged down Washington Street, a car slowed down alongside him. It was Rod Garcia's black BMW. "Hey, Sandoval," Garcia shouted out the window. "What are you running from? Did you rip off some stuff at the twenty-four-seven store or the deli? Is some shopkeeper coming after you?"

Ernesto kept on jogging, ignoring Garcia. He stared straight ahead, pretending Garcia wasn't even there. But Garcia wouldn't give up. "You better watch yourself, Sandoval. If you're swiping stuff from the stores, they won't let you stay on as senior class president. Nobody wants some dirty little thief representing the class," Garcia yelled.

Ernesto refused even to turn his head.

"What'd you steal, man?" Garcia taunted. "Some razors? Maybe one of those little bottles of whiskey. They're easy to snatch. You look like the kind of homie who likes to drink."

Ernesto wanted to turn and tell Rod Garcia to drop dead. But Ernesto knew that doing something like that would only encourage him. Maybe if he weren't senior class president, Ernesto would have yelled something. But he had to respect the office he now held. Mrs. Sanchez, the principal at Cesar Chavez High School, made it very clear to all the candidates for school office: If they won, they would certainly have to adhere to the standards of Chavez students. But they'd also needed to go that extra mile in courtesy and good behavior. So Ernesto just thought of the catchy lyrics of his favorite new salsa tune. Focusing on that helped him drown out Garcia's voice.

Ernesto turned onto Tremayne, and he noticed the BMW was gone. Garcia had gotten tired of having a one-way conversation. Ernesto wondered about Garcia. How did such a creep get to be the head of all those fast-track school clubs? He probably would have been elected if Ernesto hadn't come along. Maybe, Ernesto thought, Garcia's well-to-do parents donated a lot of stuff to the school. Often, affluent parents donated soft drinks and refreshments for some of the school activities.

Then again, Garcia might have put on a good act just to become senior class president. He was the good guy who ran the environmental club. He was willing to deal with all those sticky donated cola cans for the good of the planet. Rod probably hid his true character, as real politicians sometimes did until they got elected. Now Rod had nothing to lose, so his true self came out in all its ugliness.

When Ernesto got to Wren Street, he turned. As he jogged up his driveway, he noticed a familiar car parked there. It was his grandmother on his mom's side, Eva Vasquez. She and Grandfather Alfredo lived in a nice gated community in Los Angeles. They managed to visit at least once a month.

Ernesto tried to like Grandmother Eva, but he was never happy to see her. She had had big dreams for Maria, Ernesto's mom. She wanted her only child, Maria Vasquez, to go to college and then to graduate school. She pictured her daughter getting a job in a prestigious company where she would quickly become the CEO. Mom was very smart. She had a 4.50 grade point average in high school. She would have excelled in college. And she probably would have fulfilled her mother's dream if she hadn't met Luis Sandoval.

Grandma Eva was not thrilled about her daughter marrying Luis. At the time, he was a poor college student who was about to become an ill paid high school teacher. College, grad school, the vision of a big desk on Madison Avenue—Maria traded it all in for marriage and staying home to raise kids. Grandma Eva was especially grieved by the new Sandoval baby, little Alfredo. She had hoped her daughter's childbearing and raising days were over. Maybe she might yet get that college degree, but it was not to be.

Ernesto stood at the door, leaning his forehead against it. He'd just had to put up with Rod Garcia. Now Grandma Eva was ready to spread disharmony in the Sandoval home. It hadn't been Ernesto's best day so far, and it stood to get worse.

CHAPTER TWO

Y͏ou're young, darling," Grandma Eva was telling Ernesto's mother. "But you look old and weary before your time! You look so awful!"

Ernesto had just opened the door. Something in his grandmother's voice, combined with his memory of Rod Garcia's abuse, triggered an irrational reaction.

"Mom looks hot!" Ernesto almost shouted. "Everybody at school says she's the hottest mom of them all. At senior orientation the other night, my friends said she looked like a senior girl instead of a mom."

Maria Sandoval looked at her eldest son in shock. Then she dissolved in girlish giggles. Ernesto really did think his mother was amazingly beautiful. Even though she was busy with three kids and a newborn, she looked terrific. Grandma Eva was all wet.

"Ernesto!" Grandma Eva scolded. "You do not refer to your mother as 'hot.' That is disrespectful. At any rate, you know that little Al is running her ragged. Now she doesn't even have time for her children's books."

Grandma's tone became wistful. "She's been turned into a drudge. Cooking, cleaning. Why she's little better than a maid! I thought by now your mother would be rising in the corporate world. Now she scarcely has enough time to write her little books."

Ernesto asked, "How is *Abuelo* Alfredo? Little Alfredo's namesake. Did you get those cute photos on your computer? I bet *Abuelo* Alfredo liked them!"

Grandmother Eva glared at her grandson. "Your grandfather is all right," she sniffed. When Ernesto was born, he was given his other grandfather's middle name. Grandfather Vasquez felt slighted. Now the situation was remedied with the birth of little Alfredo, his namesake. Grandma Eva wanted the baby christened Alfred, but he was christened Alfredo.

Mom knew what Ernesto was up to. She brought the conversation back to the original subject.

"Mom, I'm really okay," Maria Sandoval said. "It's getting easier every day. Ernie helps with the cleaning, and the girls entertain the baby. I'll be getting at my books again any day now. I've got lots of ideas."

"*Abuela*," Ernesto began, looking directly at his grandmother. He knew full well she didn't like to be called "*abuela*." "I saw something really incredible coming home from school the other day. It was in a field. I saw this lizard with a brilliant blue tail. He was climbing on some rocks in a field on Bluebird Street. Maybe Mom could write a children's book about it."

"Honestly, Ernesto," Grandma Eva snorted, "there are no such things as lizards with blue tails. Sometimes you don't even seem like a seventeen-year-old, Ernesto. You're more like a seven-year-old making up childish stories."

Ernesto strode to the encyclopedia that nobody looked at anymore because everything could be found online. He flipped pages until he came to a photograph of a creature with a blue tail. "See here?" Ernesto said. "The common western skink. It has a cool blue tail."

The older woman sighed, looked at her expensive watch, and rose from the chair. "Well, I have to run. I'll see you soon, dear." She embraced her daughter and advised, "Do take care of yourself. Don't get old before your time running around for the child. Get some help. Surely you people can afford help, and, if not, I—"

"No, no, Mom. We're fine," Ernesto's mother insisted, holding the door for her.

She waved to her mother as she went to her car.

As Eva Vasquez was backing her car out of the driveway, Mom turned to Ernesto. "Ernie, you weren't on your best behavior, you know. You were a little rude," she scolded.

"I know, Mom. I'm sorry," Ernesto apologized. "It's been kind of a rugged day. You know that guy I beat out of senior class president, Rod Garcia? Well, he confronted me this morning like a rattlesnake. He really hates me for getting the job. He thought he had it coming to him."

"Oh, honey," Mom said, "that's awful. I don't know the family well, but I thought the boy had more class than that."

"Yeah, I didn't know the guy before this," Ernesto said. "I guess he's been planning all through high school to be senior class president. He joined cubs, made himself important. He was so sure of winning, he didn't even campaign hard. He seemed to think he'd inherit the job. He figured the world owed him, like it owed him a BMW at seventeen.

Mom stared at her son in disbelief. "Anyway," Ernesto went on, "I get to be the dirty rat who stole the golden boy's crown. He told me all my friends were gang-bangers. He said all my relatives up in LA were probably serving time in prison. He said he hoped I flunked all my classes. He was back at it just now, when I was jogging home. He was driving alongside me, yelling insults. He said I probably just ripped off the deli, and that's why I was running."

"My goodness!" Mom gasped. "What an awful person. Did you tell your friends what happened?"

"Yeah. I told Abel and Naomi and Carmen," Ernesto answered. "You can trust them not to go nuts. But Garcia was dissing Paul Morales too, calling him a thug. I wouldn't tell him that. Paul's kind of a loose cannon."

Nine-year-old Katalina was standing in the doorway to the living room. Ernesto had not seen his sister until just now, but she had been listening. She now had serious look on her pretty little face.

Katalina remarked, "That guy must really be mean. Your friends aren't gang-bangers, but they're kinda funny. The other day, me and Juanita and Dad were coming home from the market. You were standing by a car full of guys, a low rider. Everybody was laughing and yelling. The car was jumping up and down like a kangaroo. And every time it jumped, a big 'oogah' horn went off. Me and Juanita thought it was funny, but Dad looked kinda funny . . ."

Ernesto felt like laughing, but he didn't. "They're nice guys, Kat. Really they are. Paul's the manager of a big computer store, and his boss trusts him with everything. Cruz and Beto, they're studying the building trades. Dom and Carlos are seniors now. They're gonna finish high school and go to the community college. They were just, you know, having fun with the car."

"Why does Paul have that rattlesnake tattooed on his hand again?" Katalina asked. "I forget."

"His buddies, Cruz and Beto, were with him in the desert one time," Ernesto explained. "A rattlesnake bit him. He could've died if they hadn't carried him to where the paramedics met them. It saved his life. He put the tattoo on there so he'd never forget what his friends did for him."

"Oh yeah!" Katalina recalled. "I like it when he moves his fingers and makes the rattlesnake jump."

The next day, after classes, Ernesto had to meet with the teacher in charge of senior activities. She would coordinate with him on class meetings and big projects coming up. Ernesto had a big project of his own. He wanted to set up senior mentors for kids who were having academic problems. He wanted to make sure nobody dropped out before graduation because they couldn't make the grade. Ernesto's main concern was finding enough good-hearted seniors who would volunteer their time to help struggling fellow students. Ernesto believed that many kids wouldn't go to a teacher or even an adult for help but would turn to a peer.

The other big project was the homecoming dance and the selection of homecoming king and queen. The king and queen would be crowned at the homecoming dance after the big football game that day. Ernesto dreaded kids vying for the positions.

Deprise Wilson was the senior art teacher and the senior activities advisor. Ernesto was scheduled to meet her today. It would be the first time he had a chance to speak with her.

After classes, Ernesto went into Ms. Wilson's office. She was a beautiful young black woman with a bubbly personality. She looked scarcely older than the seniors. She flashed her huge smile and said, "Sit down, Ernie. Oh, I've heard so many good things about you. I'm really excited to be working with you. Two of your friends are in my art class, Dom Reynosa and Carlos Negrete. They told me this amazing story about once being taggers and high school dropouts. Then you and your father turned them around, got them back in school. So they're the ones who did that amazing mural of Cesar Chavez and his friends here at school. Actually Ernie, those boys worship you!"

Ernesto was embarrassed. "Actually," he mumbled, "most of the credit for helping those guys goes to my dad and my friend, Abel Ruiz. They're the ones who should get the credit."

"Ah yes, Luis Sandoval, your father." Ms. Wilson gushed. "What a marvelous teacher he is. The students just love him, and he knows his history. He's an amazing teacher."

Ms. Wilson seemed nice, but her enthusiasm was making Ernesto dizzy. "So," he started to say, "we're having this senior class meeting in the auditorium on Thursday. We'll talk about getting a core group of seniors who are willing to tutor other seniors. And we'll also get the ball rolling on the homecoming stuff. We'll need to get a theme for the dance. How's that sound, Ms. Wilson?"

"Oh, Ernie, you are so organized and so enthusiastic," Ms. Wilson told him. "And it's only the first week of school. This is so amazing! I'm so excited. I just know we're going to have such an amazing year at Chavez. I'm going to enjoy working with you so much."

"Yeah, well, I'll be glad to work with you too," Ernesto responded. "It'll be all good." Ernesto smiled and left the office. He felt as though he'd just had a conversation with a spinning cotton candy machine.

When Ernesto closed the door behind him, he noticed Naomi Martinez waiting for him.

"So, do you like her?" Naomi asked.

"Uh . . . she's different . . . she's nice," Ernesto replied.

Naomi giggled. "You poor thing. You didn't know what to make of her. She's really pretty, and she's like still in middle school, you know?'

"Yeah, she's got a lot of spirit. Yeah . . . everything is—" Ernesto started to say.

"Amazing," Naomi finished his sentence, giggling again.

Ernesto laughed. "You got that right. Hey, why don't we try that new frappé place across the street? Abel said the fraps are really good," he suggested.

"You're on," Naomi agreed, slipping her soft hand into Ernesto's. Her touch never ceased to give Ernesto goose bumps.

"So, how do you like your classes so far, Naomi?" Ernesto asked as they crossed Washington.

"I like Mr. Ardith in biology," Naomi answered. "He knows so much. And it's important for me to have good science classes because that's what I'll be majoring in in college."

At the shop, they found a booth and sat down. Naomi looked pensive for a moment. Ernesto recognized the look. He guessed something was wrong at home.

"So, what's up?" he asked her.

"My brothers, Orlando and Manny, they came to visit last night," Naomi explained. Her brothers were in the music business in Los Angeles. Orlando sang with a Latin band. "They got into a big argument with Dad. Zack is working with Dad at the construction site. Dad's really on top of him all the time, criticizing his friends, angry when he hangs out. Zack snuck off and got drunk with his buddies, and Dad slapped him. That really burned Orlando and Manny. Luckily, I was able to quiet things down. Most of the time Dad's okay, but sometimes that ugly temper comes out."

Years ago, Mr. Martinez had slapped his wife. Orlando and his father had had an especially bitter argument, and Orlando decked his dad. When Ernesto began dating Naomi, her parents were completely estranged from Orlando and Manny. Naomi, with Ernesto's help, arranged for the boys to reconcile with Mr. Martinez. Naomi loved her brothers and had missed them. Her mother had been broken hearted during the estrangement.

Suddenly, somebody was standing at the booth where Ernesto and Naomi were drinking their frappés. They hadn't seen Clay Aguirre come in, and he was the last person either of them wanted to see now. He was the always the last person they wanted to see.

Naomi had no more feeling for Clay, but she tried to be polite. She would never forget his violent slap across the face, but she tried to forgive him. She even felt sorry for him because he was an unhappy person. He was struggling to bring up his grade point average so that he could return to his passion—football. He had a nasty personality, so he alienated most of the kids. He didn't even have a girl-friend now.

"Hi, Clay," Naomi forced herself to smile thinly.

"Hi, Naomi," Clay responded, his gaze going quickly to Ernesto. "Hey, dude, I think a lot of the seniors are wishing they could take back their votes. I think they'd like to get somebody else for senior class president. I mean, you're already showing up as pretty lame, man. You hear what I'm saying?"

"No, Clay," Naomi pleaded softly. "Let's just be—"

"It was one of those elections, you know," Clay continued, ignoring Naomi's plea. "Kids got carried away with all your phony rhetoric, man. You just swept them off their feet. But you're all flash and no substance. You're an empty suit, dude. You're like that guy in *The Wizard of Oz*. There's nothing behind the curtain. Now they're taking a good look, and they know they picked a loser. Now they're stuck with you. Too bad we don't have recalls."

"Well, like they say," Ernesto said, smiling and sipping his frappé, "stuff happens."

"Rod Garcia, now there was a guy who could have been a great senior class president," Clay rattled on. "For three years now, he's been running just about everything. You wanted something done, he was the go-to guy. He would have made this year the best senior year a class ever had."

Ernesto and Naomi were doing their best to ignore the taunt. Ernesto kept the advice of Mrs. Sanchez in mind: "Go that extra mile in courtesy and good behavior."

"Now what have we got?" Clay went on. "A screwup who hangs with guys with one foot in prison and the other foot on a banana peel. I can't wait till the cops do a sweep of the gangbangers. Maybe they'll pull you in with the rest of your homies, man. Then how is that gonna look for our school?"

Ernesto and Naomi were finished with their frappés. Ernesto announced, "Well, much as I'm enjoying this pep talk, I think we'll split, right, babe?"

"Totally," Naomi agreed, starting to get up.

But Clay blocked their path. "It's not just me talking, man," he snarled. "A lotta the students are feeling the same way. They got buyers' remorse, big time. You're gonna mess up bad, Sandoval. You're not gonna be able to lead the seniors. Nobody's gonna want to listen to you. When all is said and done, you're just a wimpy nobody from LA. You got a big head and bit off more than you could ever chew. When you stand up in front of that senior class on Thursday for the first meeting, your legs are gonna turn to water, man. You're gonna start shaking. The real wimp is gonna be standing there naked in fronta his enemies—*a lot of enemies*, believe me."

"Just get out of our way, Clay," Naomi commanded. "We're tired of all this nonsense. We got better things to do than listen to a sorehead." Naomi's voice was bitter, even though she had tried to be polite.

Ernesto and Naomi walked for a long time after exiting the coffee shop. They talked about everything but nothing important. They just enjoyed being together. And

Ernesto was especially glad to be holding her hand for a while.

Before they parted for the night, Naomi put her arms around Ernesto and asked softly, "You okay, babe?" She knew what Ernesto was going through, even though she could put it into words.

"Sure," Ernesto responded, smiling at the girl.

Naomi kissed Ernesto on the lips, and a tremor of joy went through his body. Usually Naomi's tenderness could make all the darkness go away, but tonight it didn't work completely.

When Ernesto got home, his sisters were doing their homework with *Abuela* Lena's help. Mom was giving little Alfredo a bath, and Dad was preparing a history test for his juniors. "Hi, *mi hijo*," Dad greeted. Ernesto needed to talk to his father, but he didn't want to disturb him. But Luis Sandoval got up, got his sweater, and said, "It's a beautiful night for a walk, Ernie. Let's go."

39

CHAPTER THREE

Look at the moon," Luis Sandoval pointed as they reached the sidewalk. "A perfect shining crescent. Looks like you could put a baby in it and rock him to sleep."

"Dad, how did you know?" Ernesto asked in wonder.

"That it was time for a walk, just you and me? I've known you for a long time, *mi hijo*," Ernesto's father replied with a smile. "What's up?"

His father could always take a look at Ernesto and know something was wrong. Luis Sandoval was so close to his son that, when the boy's heart ached, the father felt the pain.

Ernesto told his father about Rod Garcia's angry tirade against him and what Clay Aguirre had said. Then the boy added ruefully, "I'm seventeen years old. I'm almost a man. I should be able to handle stuff like this. Why do I let this garbage get to me? I feel like a wimp. Where's the *macho* in me?"

Dad put his arm around his son's shoulders. "No, no, don't be so hard on yourself," Dad consoled him. "We're all programmed to expect civility from other people. It shakes us when somebody comes on with raw hatred. Deep down, you're strong, Ernie, but you are only human. Being attacked hurts."

Ernesto guessed that his father had had Rod Garcia in classes during his junior year. Clay Aguirre too. He had probably formed some opinion of them. Dad wouldn't share that with Ernesto, and Ernesto did not expect him to. Luis Sandoval was totally professional. He was respectful of his students' privacy. What happened in the classroom stayed there. Ernesto respected him for that. A few times, Ernesto had passed the teachers lounge at Cesar Chavez High, and he'd heard the teachers joking about some of their students. He didn't like that.

"You know what, Dad?" Ernesto remarked. "It's the thought of Thursday when I'm standing in front of all those kids at the senior class meeting. I'm afraid I'm gonna freeze and make an idiot of myself. I'm afraid I'll just be staring at Garcia and Aguirre, and they'll be doubled over laughing. I think that's what's really got to me."

"Ernie, here's a trick," the father advised. "I learned it a long time ago in college when I had to make presentations before groups during my student teaching days. You find a friendly face in the audience, or a couple of them, and you talk to them. They're your focus. When other students raise their hands for a question, look at them momentarily, and reply to the question. Then get your focus back on your friends. It'll get easier and easier, *mi hijo*."

His father sounded very sure of what he was saying. Dad put his arm around Ernesto's shoulders and spoke quietly. "Not everybody will like you, Ernie. But the vast majority of the kids will want to give you a fair chance."

"Yeah," Ernesto said. "Abel and Naomi, Carmen, the guys from the track team, Carlos and Dom, they'll all be there. I guess I could do that, Dad. I could look at them."

Then Ernesto asked, "But, Dad, why is Rod being such a creep about this? It was a fair election. We both campaigned, and he could have won. Why can't he accept what happened?"

Luis Sandoval laughed. "Ernie," he chuckled, "look at the president who sits in the White House! This president was fairly elected. Then, the moment the oath of office is taken, the members of the other party sharpen their knives. They hack away at the man's motives, reputation, everything. It doesn't matter who the president is. If the president isn't from your party, you must attack."

They walked a few steps before Luis Sandoval went on. "Rod Garcia wanted to win, and he didn't. You did. So you're the enemy. Garcia wants you to fail to prove how wrong everybody was who voted for you. Just like in Washington. The out party wants the president to screw up so that they can get back in the next time around. Unfortunately, what happens to the nation is not important. For Garcia, what happens to the school is not important. To the losers, only winning is important. It's sad, but it's human nature. Many of us cannot rise above our own ambitions, our own selfishness."

"Yeah," Ernesto agreed. "I guess I should have learned that when we worked to get Carmen's dad elected to the city council. The people who wanted Monte Esposito attacked Mr. Ibarra all the time. They're still at it, even though Mr. Ibarra is doing a great job."

As they walked up Wren Street to Tremayne, Ernesto and his father met a girl coming their way. Ernesto recognized her from AP History. There were so few students in that class that Ernesto noticed every one.

The girl was very slender, even to the point of looking a little unhealthy. Her hair was long and straight. Even though it was a balmy evening, she wore a heavy long-sleeved hoodie. She was walking very fast, as if she didn't want to speak with anybody. Ernesto recalled that she always wore long sleeves in class too. Maybe, he thought, she wanted to hide how thin her arms were.

As Ernesto and his father neared her, the girl glanced at them. She seemed to recognize Ernesto, but she blinked, lowered her head, and hurried on. Ernesto customarily said "Hi" to anybody he met face to face on the street even if he didn't know them. It seemed rude not to recognize the girl. But she seemed so determined not to get involved that he let it go.

Luis Sandoval noticed that Ernesto was perplexed. He asked, "Do you know her?"

"Yeah, she's in my AP History class," Ernesto explained. "I felt weird not saying 'hi' or anything."

"She seemed in a hurry," Ernesto's father remarked.

Ernesto and his father turned down Bluebird Street, where Naomi Martinez lived. Sometimes she was out watering the rose bushes or something, or even walking Brutus, the family's pit bull. Ernesto always hoped he might get a glimpse of her. Anytime Ernesto got the chance to see Naomi was a big plus for him.

The Sandovals usually sauntered down Bluebird, then worked their way back up Wren toward home. But as they neared the Martinez house, they heard angry shouting. Luis Sandoval glanced sadly at his son. "Uh-oh," Dad commented. "It sounds like Felix Martinez is on the warpath again. You can hear his voice on the whole street. He's giving the whole neighborhood a show."

"You ain't goin' nowhere, you lousy bum," Mr. Martinez was screaming. The front door of the house was open, and Ernesto could see who was being yelled at. It was Felix Martinez's youngest son—Zack.

Last year, Mr. Martinez had wanted Zack to go to college, but the boy insisted on joining his father on the construction site as an apprentice. They battled over the question for a long time. Felix Martinez finally gave in, but now another problem was surfacing.

Mr. Martinez and his son were together too much. Felix Martinez wasn't giving the boy room to breathe. Zack needed time away with his friends. But a few times Zack came home drunk, and that infuriated his father. Felix Martinez had struggled with the bottle himself, and he didn't want his son going down that road.

"Oh man!" Ernesto muttered. They were standing only a few feet from the Martinez house. "You think we could do anything,

Dad? Poor Naomi and her mom. They must be so upset. Look, some of the neighbors are outside watching!"

"Felix Martinez doesn't take too kindly to other people interfering in his family," Luis Sandoval replied.

But the fight was getting worse. Felix Martinez was holding his son by the shoulders. Zack broke free and shouted, "You're not stopping me from being with my friends. You got no right. I'm a man. I'm not some little punk kid. I got a right to hang out with my friends."

Zack sprinted down the walk with his father in hot pursuit. Felix Martinez grabbed the boy and shouted, "You ain't going out there to drink yourself stupid, boy. If I gotta take the belt to you, then I'll do that too!"

Zack wrenched away from his father, sending the older man sprawling on the sidewalk. Zack looked like he'd already had too much to drink.

"Oh boy!" Luis Sandoval groaned. "We've got to get into it now, Ernie. Felix is getting up. There's going to be a brawl, and somebody could get hurt. You take Zack." The Sandovals sprinted up the driveway of the Martinez house.

Linda Martinez was in the doorway now, screaming for her husband and son to stop fighting. Neither her husband nor her son was paying any attention to her.

Ernesto and his father rushed up just as Zack threw a punch at his father, almost sending him down again. Ernesto grabbed Zack in a bear hug, pinning his arms to his sides. He dragged Zack away from his father, who was ready to swing at his son. Luis Sandoval grabbed Felix Martinez and pulled him back as well.

"Felix, stop it!" Luis Sandoval shouted. "Everybody on the street is out watching! Next thing you know, the cops'll be here. You and the boy'll be hauled off! Do you want that?"

"You mind your own business, Sandoval," Felix Martinez fumed, trying to pull free of the younger, stronger man. "What're you doin' stickin' your nose in another man's business? Who the devil do you think you are? A man has the right to take care of his own kid!"

Luis Sandoval's mouth was near the man's ear. He didn't have to shout. Quietly, he said, "Yes, Felix, but not like this. Not in front of everyone." Mr. Sandoval felt the man relax in his grip.

Linda Martinez was now sobbing. "Zack, please come inside and go to your room. Please, Zack, do it for me."

Naomi appeared then, her face disfigured with hurt and shame. "Zack, you're better than this! Do it for Mom, please!"

Zack cursed as he shook himself free of Ernesto and walked back inside the house. Even outside, they heard his bedroom door slam, causing the small house itself to tremble.

Ernesto's father released Felix Martinez, who stood there trembling with rage. "It's her fault," he declared. "That fool of a wife I got. Last time the kid acted up, I wanted to give him a good whippin', but she stopped me. His brothers too. They took the kid's side. They all turned against me—Orlando, Manny, my own wife."

The man was raving in a loud voice. "They stopped me from disciplinin' my own kid. Zack needs to be whipped so hard that he can't sit down for a week. He's gotta learn more respect. A man has the right to train up his own son so he don't go rotten. But she won't let me, that weak, stupid woman I got in there." Mr. Martinez wound up standing in a slight crouch, pointing an accusing finger at his wife.

Then Felix Martinez's eyes narrowed, and he turned his wrath on Luis Sandoval. "You didn't need to come charging up like the U.S. Marines, Sandoval. If you'd stayed outta it, I woulda whipped some decency into the kid. What makes you think you got the right? You jus' come flyin' in here and take charge of another man's business."

51

Naomi hurried to her father's side. "Daddy," she told him, "it was out of control, and you know it. Everybody on the street is out watching. Maybe they already called the police. This is so awful. Thank God Ernie and his father came along to calm things down."

Ernesto felt so sorry that Naomi had to be in the middle of this. He knew how embarrassed she must be. The Torres family lived right across the street, and their daughter, Roxanne, was the gossip of the senior class at Chavez. Roxanne loved to gossip. By tomorrow morning, this incident would be all over the school.

"Look, Felix," Luis Sandoval explained, "I didn't want to get involved. But you guys were having at each other so bad I was afraid somebody would get hurt. Why don't you just go inside, have a cup of coffee, and calm down?"

"Listen to him!" Felix Martinez snarled loudly. "He's talking to me like he talks to some little punk in his classroom down at Chavez. I'm a man, Sandoval." Mr. Martinez thumped his chest with the palm of his hand. "I don't take a scolding from some wimpy teacher who thinks he knows it all."

He spun on his heel and stalked into his house, slamming the door behind him. He left the Sandovals and Naomi out on the sidewalk. The neighbors disappeared back into their houses. The show was over. Gladly, no police cruisers showed up.

"Of all the males in our household," Naomi remarked, "I think Brutus is the only well behaved one." A rueful look filled her eyes. "If only Daddy and my brothers were as nice as that pit bull!"

Ernesto hugged Naomi and consoled her. "Take it easy, babe. It'll be okay."

A small smile crept into Naomi's violet eyes. She looked right at Luis Sandoval and said, "You raised a winner here, Mr. Sandoval."

Ernesto's father smiled. "You just hang in there, Naomi. This too will pass," he advised.

Naomi started back to the house. Ernesto and his father continued their way toward home. Luis Sandoval remarked, "Naomi's a wonderful girl."

"Yeah, and she's had to go through a lot," Ernesto said.

At school the next morning, Ernesto spotted the tall, slender girl they'd met last night on the walk. He'd been reluctant to say "Hi" to her last night, but this time he smiled at her and spoke. "Hi. You're in AP History too, aren't you?"

"Ah yes," she replied.

"I guess you're a walker too," Ernesto commented. "Me and my dad passed you last night on our walk, didn't we?"

"Ah yes, I think so," she responded.

"I'm Ernesto Sandoval," he introduced himself. "There are so few students in AP History, we'll probably be doing projects together."

The girl hesitated before saying, "I'm Bianca Marquez. I'm not sure I'll stay in the class. I'm a pretty good student, but it seems really hard."

"Yeah," Ernesto agreed, "it strikes me as hard too, but I want that college credit. I think we can do it. We could even study together if you'd like. That always helps. My *abuela*—she lives with us—she says two heads are better than one."

"You . . .," Bianca noted, suddenly staring at Ernesto, "you're senior class president, aren't you?"

"Yeah. It shocks me sometimes when I wake up and realize what I got myself into," Ernesto admitted. "I never dreamed of running for the office, but my friends sorta pushed me into it."

"I remember the campaign speech you gave," Bianca remarked. "I don't remember what the other guy who was running said, or what the girl said. But you said you wanted to start this mentoring program where the seniors would help each other. You sounded like you really cared about everybody. It sort of blew me away, and I voted for you."

"Thanks," Ernesto said.

"I voted for you, but I didn't expect you would be . . . you know, like you are. I thought anybody who ran for senior class president would be stuck up, but you're just a regular guy," Bianca said.

"I *am* just a regular guy, but I'll sure try my best to do a good job," Ernesto said.

At midday, Ernesto was standing in front of the vending machine, trying to decide between a peach and a pear. Both fruits looked so good.

"The pear looks better," Naomi suggested. Ernesto had not seen her come up alongside him. "Looks juicy."

Ernesto turned and grinned. "I think you're right," he said. He slipped his money into the machine, pressed the button, and got his pear.

"Uh . . . everything settle down at home, babe?" he asked.

"Sort of," Naomi replied.

Just then there was a burst of laughter by the sandwich machine, about twenty-five feet away. From the corner of her eye, Naomi recognized her neighbor from across the street, Roxanne Torres. The Torres family had lived in their house on Bluebird Street for about three years now. But they never became close friends with any of the neighbors. They rarely took part in any of the neighborhood activities. Mr. Torres worked all the time. Mrs. Torres seemed to believe that her family was a cut above the other people on the street. She didn't try to socialize.

Roxanne was a cute, popular girl, who loved to gossip. She tweeted and texted everything she saw, especially embarrassing things. Some of the girls at Chavez were a little overweight. Roxanne made it a point to take photos of them from behind and send the pictures to her friends.

Right now Roxanne was sharing something on her iPhone that was creating quite a stir. Her friends giggled and squealed with delight.

Ernesto noticed hurt on Naomi's face, and his heart sank. He wondered whether Roxanne had taken pictures of what happened at the Martinez house last night.

"That's her father," Roxanne announced loudly, followed by a fresh burst of laughter. Her friends crowded in for a better look. "That's her brother. Wow, it was like fight night at the gorilla park at the zoo."

Ernesto stared at Naomi, his heart breaking. She seemed near tears.

"Ernie," Naomi gasped, "she took pictures last night, and she'll put them online! I know it. We'll be the laughingstocks of the whole city!" Naomi looked pale and shaken.

Ernesto sprinted over to where Roxanne and her friends were gathered. Ernesto had two classes with Roxanne last year. They weren't friends, but they got along. "Hey, Roxie," he asked. "What've you got there?"

Roxanne looked a little nervous. "Uh . . . nothing . . .," she replied, turning red.

Ernesto could see the images of Felix Martinez and Zack struggling on the iPhone. He could imagine it going viral on the Internet.

"Roxie," Ernesto commanded in a calm, stern voice, "lose that stuff. Delete it. I'm not kidding you. You and your friends have had a laugh over it, but that's the end of it. If you put those pictures out online, you're violating that guy's privacy. He could sue you. He could sue your family and take your house away from you."

The girl blinked at Ernesto, glanced down at the iPhone, and looked back at him.

"I'm serious, Roxie," Ernesto told her. "My uncle is a lawyer, and he's the kind of do-gooder who would take the case. He'd do it just to make a point. You'll be in a world of trouble if you don't just delete it right now and be done with it."

Roxanne Torres was not a very smart girl, and she was easily frightened. She wasn't a bad person, just someone who liked to gossip twenty-four-seven.

"Oh, I wasn't going to put it out there, Ernie," she said quickly. "I was just showing it to a couple friends . . . it's kinda funny . . ."

"Get rid of it, Roxie," Ernesto insisted. "You don't want to bring a lawsuit on your family, right?" He kept his voice soft and commanding.

"There," Roxanne replied, "I deleted it, Ernie."

When Ernesto went back to where Naomi stood, she threw her arms around him and hugged him. "My hero! My knight in shining armor!"

"No big deal," Ernesto responded. "Roxie'll be gossiping about it all day. But at least the pictures won't be making the rounds."

CHAPTER FOUR

After the last class of the day, Ernesto headed for the school auditorium for his first senior class meeting. A lot of his friends were heading in the same direction, and they cheered him. But he had no illusions about what might happen. Rod Garcia and Clay Aguirre would be there too. They would do everything they could to make Ernesto look bad.

Ernesto remembered his father's advice: Focus on the friendly faces.

About fifty students were sitting there as Ernesto walked in. The secretary and other senior officers were already there, along with Ms. Wilson. Before long, more than a hundred students were in the auditorium.

When Ernesto opened the meeting, he heard somebody snicker, but he ignored it.

"Hi," Ernesto began. "You all know who I am, and you know we've got a lot of work to do."

Clay Aguirre yawned loudly and stretched, creating a little pool of laughter. Ernesto ignored the weak feeling in his knees and continued. "The first order of business is that we need to find a theme for the homecoming dance. Anybody with an idea, just fill out one of the blue cards on the table by the doors and stick it in one of the boxes. Later on we'll be electing the homecoming king and queen, but right now all we need is a theme."

Rod Garcia raised his hand.

"Yeah?" Ernesto said, glancing at Rod who was sneering.

"You need to take some speech therapy, man. A lot of us can't hear you and you don't sound very inspiring," Rod heckled.

"Yeah," Clay Aguirre chimed in. "You sound like you're dead and don't know it."

A rumble of annoyance at the remarks echoed through the auditorium. It came from Ernesto's friends and from students who didn't like the mean-spirited cracks.

Ernesto looked at the two wise guys and replied, "Thank you for your opinions."

Then I looked again at his friends and continued. "Now, when I ran for senior class president, I promised to do all I could to help kids who are struggling. Whether they were having academic or other problems, we'd have a student outreach for them. That's what I'm really concerned about getting started today. I'm putting out the call to any seniors who'd be willing to mentor or tutor. We'll also take any seniors who will just be friends to other schoolmates who're having a hard time."

For the moment, the hall was quiet. From the audience, Naomi smiled at Ernesto, who smiled back. "A lot of times," Ernesto went on, "kids in trouble won't reach out to a teacher and maybe not even their parents, but they'd let a peer help them. If you'd like to be a part of this, I'm passing out sign-up lists right now. I need your name, phone number, e-mail. We'll organize into an informal band of *compañeras* and *compañeros*."

"Aw, that's really sweet," Clay Aguirre cooed. "Losers helping losers."

"I think it's a really lame idea," Rod Garcia agreed in a loud voice.

Deprise Wilson stood up from her place in the rear of the auditorium. "Clay, Rod, you're out of order. You didn't ask to be recognized to speak. Furthermore, snide remarks are not going to get anything worthwhile done."

Applause swept the auditorium.

When quiet had returned, Yvette Ozono raised her hand. Ernesto recognized her, and she stood up and spoke. "You guys, I've got something to say about how a student can help someone else." Yvette's voice was strong and passionate. "I don't even think I'd be alive right now if it wasn't for Ernesto and his friends. Some of you know my story, but for those of you who don't, let me tell it. I'd dropped out of Chavez, and I was a gang girl. When I got outta the gang and started dating a good kid, Tommy Alvarado, my old boyfriend murdered Tommy. I sunk so low I didn't want to live anymore."

Yvette glanced and nodded toward Ernesto. She turned back to the audience and went on. "Ernesto and his father came to my apartment where Mom and me and my little brothers and sisters lived. They convinced me to hang in there. When I got back to Chavez, a lotta the kids shunned me, but Ernesto and his friends helped me. Helped me so much. I was eating lunch with a friendly group of kids that first day back, and I had hope again. Naomi Martinez and Abel Ruiz and Carmen Ibarra—they all reached out to me and cared. They put their arms around me, and they *saved* me. They were *compañeros* and *compañeras* for me. They were a lifeline."

Ernesto's friends were looking down at their hands, a little embarrassed by the attention. Yvette had more to say. "Now I'm doing so good here at Chavez that I've won math prizes. I'm going to college on a scholarship. I'm going to sign up for Ernesto's program to help some other senior. I want to do for somebody else what was done for me."

The whole auditorium broke out in sustained applause when Yvette sat down.

Ernesto didn't look at Clay and Rod and their friends, but he heard no noise from their direction.

Dom Reynosa raised his hand. "Same with me and my homie, Carlos—Carlos Negrete. We were dropouts hangin' on the street and taggin'. All the neighborhood cops knew us. We were turning hardcore when Abel and Ernesto got after us and dragged us back to school. Now we're doing school murals and we're not in trouble no more. We're gonna graduate, man. Who'da thought it? My old man can't believe it. That's what Ernie's talking about . . . getting kids helping kids, that's all. Just keeping our eyes open to who needs a hand, dudes."

More applause followed Dom's comments.

"Well," Ernesto said after the applause died down, "I had a big speech about the program. But I guess Yvette and Dom put it a lot better than I could. Thanks, guys. And thanks to everyone for coming."

At the end of the senior class meeting, the sign-up sheets were passed back to Ernesto. Two dozen seniors had signed up. Ernesto didn't expect them all to come through. But he was excited that so many were willing to think about it at least. Ms. Wilson came up to Ernesto as the auditorium was clearing out.

"Ernesto, that was just amazing," she gushed. "I've been to a lot of class meetings, but this was just the best. You've got this class off to a flying start. And it wasn't just the rah-rah-let's-hear-it-for-the-grand-old-team and stuff like that. Not that I have anything against sports because they're

67

great for a high school. But you put your heart into this Ernie. You touched the hearts of all the students. I'm just so proud of you. I mean, this is what it's all about, reaching out to one another and everybody getting to a goal together."

Deprise turned to Naomi and Abel, who were standing there too. "Isn't this young man just absolutely amazing?" she asked them.

"Totally," Naomi agreed.

"Yeah, right on," Abel affirmed.

Ernesto started out for his jog home late in the afternoon. He felt very good. He felt almost wonderful. Still, he didn't want to make too much of his success today for fear he couldn't keep the momentum up. He'd survived the first senior class meeting, and he'd kept it all together. He had assembled a nice group of kids who were willing to help other seniors.

As Ernesto turned the corner on Tremayne, a familiar van decorated with wildly colored symbols cruised by. It wore old peace signs, animal rights slogans, cartoons of pandas and aliens, all among strange and exotic flowers. It was a beat-up relic of the hippy era. Ernesto smiled, recognizing Paul Morales's friend, Cruz Lopez, at the wheel. Usually his friend Beto was with him, but this time he was accompanied by someone else—Zack Martinez.

"Yo, dude," Cruz shouted out to Ernesto. He slowed down and parked at the curb.

"Hey, Cruz, Zack," Ernesto hailed, going to the window. "What's going down here?"

"You know me and Beto are taking electrical courses and all kinds of construction stuff at the community college, man," Cruz explained. "Your old man got us into that, and tell 'im it's working smooth. Zack's maybe gonna join up with us. He can hang at my place."

Ernesto looked at Zack nervously. He wondered if the kid was sore about being tackled last night when he was going after his father. "Uh, sorry about last night,

Zack," Ernesto apologized. "Dad and I didn't know what to do. We just didn't want anybody hurt or, you know, the cops getting into it."

"It's okay, man," Zack responded, a hard look on his face. "You did what you thought was right. Maybe it was. But I'm outta that house on Bluebird Street."

"You talk it over with your father?" Ernesto asked.

"Are you loco, dude?" Zack almost spat out the words. "You don't talk to that dude. You take his crap, and you duck when he's coming with that belt. No more. I'm over eighteen. I'm hanging with Cruz for a while. Then who knows?"

"My old man don't care if you crash at our place," Cruz told Zack. "He works so hard, half the time he don't even know who's in the house. He's gotta support me and my little sisters. It's been hard since Ma died. Dad has to cook and wash. But pretty soon I'll be getting a job and making good money. That'll help a lot."

Cruz's mother had become ill when her husband was out of work and didn't think he had health insurance. So she waited too long to see a doctor. When she finally did, it was too late. Her disease had turned deadly.

"I got some money saved from working with my father," Zack offered. "I can pay my way." Zack opened his wallet. It looked as though it contained a lot of money. "I'm never going back to that house. My brothers split, and now I'm doing the same. You can't live with Felix Martinez."

"What'd your mother say?" Ernesto asked.

"You know her," Zack answered. "She begged me not to go. I told her I'd keep in touch. She shoulda split from him years ago. It would've been better for all of us."

"Well, good luck, Zack," Ernesto said. "Take it easy, man."

"Hey, Ernie," Zack called, "if you run into my old man, don't tell him where I am. He thinks Cruz and Beto are gangbangers, and he'd freak if he knew I was with them."

"We *are* sorta gangbangers," Cruz laughed. "But if we can make this construction stuff work, we just might go straight. You hear what I'm saying?"

"I won't blow your cover, Zack," Ernesto promised.

"Don't tell Naomi either," Zack asked. "My sister has a good heart, but she's always trying to get our family together. She's like in fantasyland. She thinks if she pulls the right strings, we can be a nice normal family. We could all have a sweet daddy who loves and respects his wife and kids. But that ain't the way Felix Martinez operates. He's like a tyrant. Everybody has to dance to his tune or else. If you cross him, you got the devil to pay. Well, I'm sick of paying."

"Well, I hope it goes okay for you," Ernesto responded.

He felt sad as the brightly colored van drove off. For several years, Linda Martinez had had no contact with her older sons. Her heart was broken. When the family reconciled, she was over the moon with happiness. Ernesto felt sorry for how she must feel now—her youngest son gone after a bitter fight. Her heart must be aching, and Naomi's heart would ache with hers.

Ernesto liked Paul Morales. He accepted Paul's close friendship with Cruz Lopez and Beto Ortiz. The guys had saved Paul's life, and he loved them like brothers. Still, Ernesto did not trust them completely. Ernesto hated to see Zack Martinez pulled into their orbit. They lived right on the thin edge between the right and wrong sides of the law.

Once, during a terrible time, there was a shooting in the barrio. Right after it, Ernesto saw Cruz Lopez running away near the scene of the crime. Ernesto was almost sure Cruz had robbed a store and gravely wounded an innocent man. Ernesto didn't go to the police out of his friendship with Paul. But he went through torment before finding out that Cruz was innocent.

Still, Ernesto hated to see Zack with Cruz. Cruz and Beto were street-smart dudes. They'd stepped outside the law more than once and gotten away with it. They did nothing serious, and nobody got hurt. But they worried Ernesto. Zack was a dumb kid, overprotected by his father. He could probably be duped into doing something that would ruin his life. Ernesto knew this new situation would bring anguish to both Naomi and her mother.

Ernesto didn't want to keep secrets from Naomi. He was completely open with her. But Zack asked him to keep his secret, and Ernesto would not go back on his word. Worse yet, if Ernesto told Naomi, she would, of course, tell her mother and maybe even her father. Protecting Zack would be paramount in her mind.

What would Felix Martinez do if he knew his youngest son was hanging out with Cruz Lopez? Ernesto wasn't sure. Maybe he'd storm over there and try to drag Zack home. As much as Ernesto hated to admit it, the father and son were violent people. Bad things could happen, and it made him sick to be in the middle of it.

Before he even got home, Ernesto got a text from Naomi. "Ernie! Zack's gone. Mom's hysterical. Call me."

Ernesto punched in Naomi's cell number. "Hey, what happened, babe?" he asked her, keeping his voice calm.

"Oh, Ernie, I got home from school," she explained, "and the place is crazy again. Dad's in a wild mood, cussing, and Mom's sobbing. While Dad was at work and Mom went to the grocery store, Zack packed his stuff and left. He didn't even leave a note. He was just so mad last night. He wouldn't talk to anybody, not even to me. We don't know where he is or anything. Dad wants to call the police, but he can't. He left here voluntarily and he's an adult." Naomi sounded very upset.

"Yeah," Ernesto agreed, "the cops aren't in the business of hauling adults back to their parents. Zack probably just went off somewhere to think. He'll probably come back in a few days."

"I don't think so, Ernie," Naomi objected. "I've never seen him so angry as he was last night. Dad's been trying to stop him from hanging with his friends, and things just kept getting worse and worse. Zack drinks, you know, and he's almost got a DUI a couple times." Ernesto could hear the pain and worry in her voice. "I don't know what to do, Ernie. You think I should call Orlando?"

"Yeah," Ernesto responded. "That's a good idea. If Orlando can get a couple days off, he'll come down with Manny. They're close to Zack. The brothers get along fine. They can maybe, you know, find him and maybe get your father to back off a little bit. Orlando can get through to your father better than anybody."

Ernesto was aching to tell Naomi that he knew where Zack was. He wasn't telling the girl he loved more than anybody else in the world. And playing dumb was making him feel very guilty.

"Ernie," Naomi said, "I called a couple of the guys Zack used to hang out with when he worked with Dad. They said they hadn't seen him. I think they were telling me the truth. Zack doesn't know anybody else. I hope he's not just living on the street or something. That'd be so dangerous. He doesn't even have a car, or he might be holed up in that."

Ernesto winced at the pain in Naomi's voice. It was like a knife twisting in his heart. "Call Orlando, babe," he urged her just before they ended the call.

When Ernesto continued jogging home, he felt perspiration leaking into his shirt. What if something happened to Zack? He'd never forgive himself if keeping Zack's secret led to something tragic.

Before he reached home, Ernesto texted Paul Morales. "Call me as soon as you can," he texted.

In two minutes, the phone rang. "Yeah, Ernie," Paul said. "What's up?"

"Paul, Naomi's brother, Zack, he left home after a big fight with his dad," Ernesto

77

explained. "Now he's staying with Cruz. I'm worried about him."

"Yeah, I know," Paul replied. "Cruz told me. The kid didn't have anywhere else to go. His old man was after him, wanting to whip him like he was ten years old. I'm tellin' you, Ernie, Felix Martinez needs to take an anger management course or something. He needs to sit down with a professional and learn how to be a good father."

"Paul," Ernesto said, "Naomi is so worried for her brother. It breaks my heart to see her like that. Zack made me promise not to blow his cover. But it's eating me alive that Naomi is so worried and I'm not telling her that Zack is okay."

"Okay, man, listen," Paul said, "I know Orlando Martinez. He's a good guy. I'll ring him up right now and tell him where Zack is. He can tell Naomi, and you're off the hook, dude. By the way, Zack's okay. Cruz's father is as good as gold. He's taking care of his family since his wife died. Nobody could ask for a better man. He wouldn't let anything happen to Zack."

"Thanks, man," Ernesto said. "More than I can say."

Ernesto waited for word from Paul, and it came in ten minutes. "Orlando has already talked to Naomi," Paul told his friend. "Orlando promised to come down and try to patch things up. Orlando told Naomi and her mom that Zack is okay and they don't need to worry. He's got a nice sleeping bag in the Lopez house. He's not hanging with the homeless guys in the ravine."

"Thanks, Paul," Ernesto said, breathing a big sigh of relief.

"Dude, anytime," Paul replied. "You're one of my favorite homies. A little too law abiding and too much of a straight shooter, but you're still okay with me."

Later in the evening, Ernesto was in his room working on a project for his AP History class. Naomi called.

"Ernie," she told him, "Paul Morales called Orlando and told him Zack's okay. He's staying in a safe place. I don't know if Paul told Orlando where Zack is or not. Orlando wouldn't say. I think he's afraid I'll tell Mom and she'll tell Dad and . . . well. Anyway I'm so glad to know that Zack has a place to sleep. I was imagining him out in the weather. It's going to rain tonight. Mom was really relieved. She isn't crying anymore. Dad is stomping around like a caged lion. Poor Brutus is hiding under the kitchen table. It's amazing how dogs can feel what's going on."

"Well, that's good news that Zack is safe anyway," Ernesto responded, still feeling guilty about keeping secrets from Naomi.

"Orlando said he's coming down to try to help," Naomi continued. "I'm so glad. If anybody can fix this mess, it's Orlando."

"That's good, babe. I like Orlando," Ernesto noted.

"Ernie, you know Paul Morales a lot better than I do," Naomi said. "I mean, Carmen Ibarra is in love with him, for heaven's sake, but . . . *do you trust him?* I mean sometimes he . . . I don't know . . . he worries me, him and his friends. Cruz and Beto. When I see them riding around in that stupid van . . . But Paul's okay, right? He wouldn't lie about Zack being in a good place, would he?"

"No, he wouldn't, Naomi," Ernesto assured her. "I do trust him. I don't think I trust any guy more. If he says Zack is okay, he's okay. It's the word."

"Okay, Ernie," Naomi replied. "That's good enough for me."

CHAPTER FIVE

Great smells were coming from the Sandoval kitchen. By the time Ernesto sat down to dinner, he almost forgot the problem with Zack Martinez.

Ernesto looked at the salmon on his plate and grinned. "Mom," he declared, "you make dinners that look and taste like they came from a five-star joint. With all you do with your books and taking care of little Alfredo and us, Mom, you're a wonder."

"She's beyond belief," Dad agreed. "And beautiful on top of it all."

Maria Sandoval laughed. "I have an ulterior motive," she confessed. "This family has got to eat healthier. Fish, salads, veggies. No *carne asada* every day. So I made cashew salmon with apricot couscous. It was really quite easy, and each serving is under four hundred calories. I don't want my handsome husband to lose his boyish figure. And I want my kids to grow up healthy too."

Ernesto tasted the salmon. "Awesome, Mom," he said, digging in for another forkful.

"You're such a good cook, Mom," Katalina said. "My best friend, Andrea, said her father doesn't have time to cook every day. So most times they get take-out food, and she's really sick of burgers and pizza."

"Poor Mr. Lopez," Mom remarked. "It must be so hard for him since his wife died. He's trying to be a father and a mother to three kids. Katalina, you should invite Andrea and Sarah over for dinner sometime. I'm sure they'd enjoy a change of pace."

"Yeah," Katalina agreed. "Maybe we should invite Cruz too, their big brother. I bet he'd like some of your good dinners,

Mom. And Zack too. Zack lives there now too."

Ernesto almost choked on his salmon.

"Zack? Zack who?" Luis Sandoval asked.

"Zack Martinez," Katalina replied. "Naomi's brother."

Maria Sandoval frowned. "That doesn't sound right. Felix Martinez would never let his boy go live with the Lopez family. He really looks down on them," she commented.

Ernesto took a deep breath. "You guys," he announced, "something bad happened at the Martinez house. You know how it was when we walked by there the other night, Dad? Well, it continued into the next day and Zack took off."

Mom's frowned deepened. "I really don't like that man, Ernie. I think the world of Naomi, but her father . . ." Her voice was troubled.

"Can I invite them all to dinner?" Katalina asked.

"Sweetheart," Mom answered carefully, "maybe you should just invite the girls—Andrea and Sarah. I can pick them up from school when I pick up you and Juanita. After dinner, I'll take them home."

"Can't I invite Cruz?" Katalina persisted.

Juanita, though younger than Katalina, was more street smart. "Kat, I think Cruz is a gang guy," she confided.

"No, he's not," Katalina objected indignantly. "Is he, Mom?"

"No, sweetheart," Mom replied again, even more carefully. "But he's . . . he's . . ." She looked at her husband for support. "What would you say Cruz Lopez is, Luis?"

"An ex-gangbanger who is now going straight and studying at the community college to make it in the building trades," Luis Sandoval answered directly.

"See?" Katalina crowed.

After dinner, Ernesto heard his parents talking in the kitchen. Ever since Alfredo had arrived, Dad was very good about helping with the after-dinner cleanup.

"Luis," Mom said softly, "Felix Martinez must be out of his mind to let his eighteen-year-old son live with the Lopez family."

"He's always a little out of his mind," Dad remarked. "But, in this case, Zack is a man and he can do as he pleases."

"You know what I mean," Mom said.

"Yes, *querida mia*," Dad responded. "The whole situation makes me sick. It's not the first time something going on in the Martinez house has done that to me."

"And Ernie, *our boy*," Mom almost wailed. "He's in the middle of it."

Ernesto winced when he heard that comment. He understood how his parents felt. They wanted good for him. They would have preferred Ernesto and Carmen Ibarra to hit it off. Now Ernesto would be with the happy, peaceful Ibarra clan. But it was not to be. Instead, Ernesto could not imagine his world without Naomi Martinez in it.

Ernesto had had a date with Naomi set for Friday night. They were going to go to the beach to take advantage of a balmy Indian summer day before winter set in. Winter was never severe, but the weather at the moment was especially lovely. But at school on Friday, Naomi said she couldn't go.

"Everything is in such turmoil at our house," the girl explained. "Orlando is coming down later tonight, and I don't know how that will go. Dad and Orlando have clashed so much before. Orlando will blame Dad for driving Zack away. Then Dad will blame Orlando for setting a bad example. I just couldn't enjoy myself at the beach with all this stuff in my head."

"Babe," Ernesto pleaded, "maybe it'd be good for you to be out of there for a few hours. It'd be so much fun at the beach. Abel's bringing Claudia, and Paul and Carmen are coming."

"I just can't, Ernie," Naomi insisted. "I'd just be thinking of what was going on at home every minute. I'd spoil it for everybody.

I'm sorry, Ernie. I was looking forward to going to the beach as much as you. Oh, Ernie, I feel so bad. I'm ruining stuff for you, and that's the last thing I want to do."

Ernesto could tell Naomi truly felt bad. "I bet sometimes you wish you'd never seen me sitting in English class that day last year in that darn pink sweater," she went on. "You deserve somebody better than me without all this family baggage. You're a winner, Ernie, and I'm a loser. I should be independent enough to let my family be and not get involved in all the drama. But . . . I love them . . . and . . ." Her voice trailed off, and she almost cried.

Ernesto put his fingers to Naomi's lips. "Don't talk like that, babe. It's wrong, and it's stupid. You're not a loser. It's not your fault that your family's going through tough times. We don't get to pick our families, Naomi. And it's not that your family isn't good, Naomi."

He put his arms around his girl and whispered his words. "Even your dad. He loves you guys, and he shows it in his way—as best he can. A lotta men, they don't care for their families a quarter as much as he does. He just doesn't know how to handle his boys. He goes nuts when he thinks he's losing control. He can't face it that his kids are growing up. When kids grow up, *all* parents lose control. It has to be that way."

Tears started running down Naomi's cheeks. "I wanted our senior year to be so good," she sniffed. "I like my classes. I'm focusing on science, and I'm doing good. I've got the nicest, sweetest, *hottest* boyfriend in the whole world. I don't want this stuff to screw it up."

"Babe, Orlando will fix things up. Trust me," Ernesto assured her. He wasn't so sure about his brave words, but he had to say something else to cheer Naomi up.

As Ernesto and Naomi started to walk from Cesar Chavez High, a short girl approached them. Ernesto didn't know her. Ernesto didn't know whether she was Rod

Garcia's girlfriend, but she was a senior and she rooted for Garcia at the track meets.

"Hi," the girl greeted them. "You don't know me. I'm Lisa Castillo. You're Naomi Martinez, aren't you?"

"Yes," Naomi replied. "I think we were in English lit class together last year. In the mixed junior-senior class?"

"Yeah," Lisa said. "Hey, I just wanted you to know that your brother Zack is hangin' out with some really bad dudes with shaved heads and tattoos. My boyfriend just texted me that he saw your brother and these gangbangers getting busted on Tremayne."

Ernesto turned cold. He put his arm around Naomi's shoulders, steadying her. "When was this?" he asked Lisa as calmly as he could.

"Just a few minutes ago. My boyfriend just texted me," the girl answered. "I looked up from my phone, and I saw you guys, and I said, 'Oh my God!' I had to tell you . . ." The girl's prattling faded out in Ernesto's mind.

Ernesto switched to his get-it-done mode. He thanked the girl and moved Naomi toward his car. He was grateful he had driven his Volvo to school today. Usually he jogged, but today was his beach date with Naomi right after school. "Come on," Ernesto said to Naomi, leading her to the parking lot. They hopped in the car, and Ernesto headed for Tremayne.

They turned the corner minutes later. Ernesto spotted two squad cars with blinking lights parked behind Cruz's garish van. Cruz, Beto, and Zack were outside the van, sitting on the curb. One officer stood by them. The other police officers were walking around the vehicle, opening doors, and looking inside.

"Oh my gosh!" Naomi whispered in a frightened voice. "What if they stole something, and now Zack is in trouble!"

Ernesto parked the Volvo a safe distance from the scene. He didn't want to spook the officers. From where they were, Ernesto and Naomi could make out what was happening. The three boys were ordered to sit on the curb while the officers searched the van.

"They're always hassling guys who look like Cruz and Beto," Ernesto said soothingly. "It's probably nothing."

"Oh, Ernie, if they arrest my brother, it'll kill Mom," Naomi groaned. "We've had our troubles, but nobody in our family has ever been arrested! Dad would have a heart attack! He's got high blood pressure anyway."

Ernesto was going to get out of the Volvo and talk to the police officers. But when he reached for the door handle, Naomi put her hand on his arm.

"No, no, Ernie!" she commanded. "If you got in trouble because of my family, I'd never forgive myself." A thought came to Naomi then. Orlando was coming down late today. Maybe he was already home. She grabbed her cell phone.

"Mom, when is Orlando—" Naomi asked.

"He's here, Naomi," Mom answered. Mom sounded relieved. "You want to talk to him? I'll put him on . . ."

"Hey, little *hermana*," Orlando got on the phone. "You okay?"

"Orlando, we're on Tremayne Street at Washington," Naomi rattled the words into the phone. "Zack and his friends are getting busted, I don't know why."

"Uh-oh," Orlando responded. "I'll grab Pop's pickup and get over there."

Within what seemed like seconds, Orlando pulled up behind Ernesto's Volvo. Naomi and Ernesto got out of the car, and Orlando embraced Naomi. He checked out the police at the van. He seemed relieved. Turning to Naomi, he said, "Looks like the cops are winding up. They check out those dudes all the time 'cause they shave their heads, wear hoodies." He looked back at the police.

The three boys got up from the curb. The police officers walked slowly away, getting into their cruisers. When Orlando,

Ernesto, and Naomi reached the van, Zack gasped, "Orlando! Man, what're you doing here?"

"Dude!" Orlando cried. "You're messing with my mind, you know that, *hermano*? You got the whole family upset, boy. You split from home, and now you're hanging around with dudes who aren't *familia*. The old man is so depressed. He's sittin' in that little house like he died already and they forgot to bury him. What's with you, *hermano*?"

"Orlando, I can't take him anymore," Zack complained. "He's on me twenty-four-seven like flypaper. Cruz said I could crash at his place." Zack nodded toward Cruz, who nodded a hello to Orlando.

"Cruz," Orlando said. "Thanks for helping my little brother, but your family has enough troubles without this crazy dude." Turning to his brother, Orlando said, "Jump in the pickup with me, Zack, and we'll talk."

"I'm not going home," Zack swore. "I can't take it anymore, man."

Orlando threw his arm around his brother's shoulders. "We'll go down to Hortencia's and have some tacos and talk. We'll work this out, *muchacho*, trust me," Orlando promised. "I never steered you wrong before, did I, Zack? I'm on your side. I love Pop, but I get where you're coming from. I been there, done that."

Zack finally got into the pickup with Orlando, and they drove off.

"Why'd the police stop you guys?" Ernesto asked Cruz.

"Some van was just seen speeding away from an ATM robbery," Cruz explained. "They tried to get the ATM machine into the van. Some joker said there was graffiti on the van, and we got lucky—we got busted. We're the usual suspects, you know."

Ernesto and Naomi drove to the Martinez house. Brutus growled a little, but his tail wagged busily when he saw Ernesto. Then Linda Martinez appeared, her eyes red from crying. Naomi went to her mother and hugged her. "Everything's okay, Mom," she assured her mother. "Orlando and Zack went to Hortencia's to talk. Orlando will take care of it."

"Oh!" Mrs. Martinez spoke in a low voice. "I've never seen your father so down, Naomi. He just sits there staring into space. Somebody called and told us that Zack had thrown in with gangbangers. I thought your father would drop dead right then and there. I think he blames himself for the whole thing with Zack."

"Where is Mr. Martinez now?" Ernesto asked.

"He's out there in the back yard in his garden," Linda Martinez replied, nodding toward the backdoor. Mr. Martinez had built the whimsical little garden years before with a waterfall and elves. It seemed so unlike the gruff, boisterous man to create a space like that. But he seemed to find peace there when he was really low.

"Let me go talk to him alone," Ernesto suggested. "He might take it better from me, Naomi, than from his little girl."

Naomi nodded. "I'll make more coffee, Mom. I think we both need it," she said.

Ernesto opened the back door. He saw Felix Martinez sitting on a stone bench, his face in his hands.

"Mr. Martinez," Ernesto spoke softly. "Mind if I join you?"

The man looked up. He looked as if he'd aged ten years in just the last few days. "Ernie, my kid's gone," the man groaned. "Little Zack. He was always the one who stuck by me, Ernie. We had that lousy fight. You saw it the other night. He wanted to go out drinkin' with those no-good bums he hangs with. I lost it, Ernie. I pictured him gettin' killed in some car crash, drivin' blind drunk. I figured some cop would be comin' to the door to tell us our boy was gone."

The man sighed deeply, his arms draped over his knees. His head was down. "I lost it, Ernie. I was too hard on the boy. I whacked him, Ernie. I shouldna done that. He cursed me. My boy cursed me. I don't think I'm ever gonna see him again. He's thrown in with some bad guys, and he's lost, Ernie. Little Zack!"

Felix Martinez said brokenly. "Orlando, he come down, but what can he do? What can anybody do now?" The man's voice shuddered in pain.

"Mr. Martinez," Ernesto began, "Orlando just picked Zack up on Tremayne Street in your pickup truck. They're going down to Hortencia's to talk. Orlando doesn't want Zack with those guys he crashed with. Cruz Lopez, he's a good guy, but Zack needs to be with his own people. He's just a kid at heart. Yeah, he's not a minor anymore, but he's not street smart. You know, Mr. Martinez, those dudes with the shaved heads and the hoodies, Zack doesn't fit in with them. Our families, yours and mine, we're different, right? Your family and mine, Mr. Martinez, we never messed with living on the edge and skipping the rules."

Ernesto's sympathetic tone brought a flicker of hope into Felix Martinez's eyes. "Yeah, Ernie, you got that right. The Sandovals and the Martinezes, we don't raise kids to do tagging and hang out on the street," Mr. Martinez declared. "We don't raise kids for prison. We don't want our kids to have rap sheets and cops always at the door. We're better than that. None of my boys ever got arrested. Not one. They ain't perfect. They been rowdy enough, but they never got arrested. I raised my boys to be honorable."

"I know you did, Mr. Martinez," Ernesto agreed. "You raised good sons. I have a lot of respect for Orlando and Manny—and Zack'll be okay too. He just needs a little maturing. You raised Naomi, the most wonderful girl I ever met, and I thank you for that."

Mr. Martinez was only half listening, bogged down in his worries. "I was too tough maybe," he said, "but you gotta fight for your kids to keep the street from takin' them away. I love my kids, Ernie. I'd die for them. I had to protect them from the streets.

You know, Ernie. You're a good kid, but you're no babe in the woods. You know a father has to fight tooth and nail for his kids, or else the street'll take 'em away."

"I know," Ernesto said—and he knew it. "The streets swallow up a lot of kids."

CHAPTER SIX

About an hour later, the pickup truck pulled into the Martinez driveway. Orlando got out first, carrying several paper bags. "Hortencia packed enough tacos for an army," he announced, coming in the front door with fragrant goods. Zack followed, carrying the salsa.

Mrs. Martinez rushed to Zack, throwing her arms around him. "I was so worried," she cried. "Are you all right?"

"Sure, Ma," Zack responded.

Orlando slapped the warm tacos and the salsa down on the table. "Everybody gather around," he ordered. "You too, Pop. We gotta have a powwow, and it goes over better with tacos and salsa. Join us, Ernie. You're almost *familia* too!"

The family and Ernesto gathered around the dining room table. Without words, everyone pitched in. They put out plates, glasses, silverware, and drinks. They put down napkins. As they did, Felix Martinez glanced nervously from Orlando to Zack. He seemed afraid. It was unusual, Ernesto thought, to see fear on his rough-hewn face.

Finally, the table was set, and the food was ready.

With everyone seat, Orlando stood up. "Pop," he announced, "you were a great father when we were all small. You were the best. You took us fishing and hiking. You played baseball and football with us. You made boys into men, and you were the best. But then, when we got to be men, not so much. You never saw those little *niños* as *hombres*, even when we got as tall as you, *Padre*, or even taller. Me and Manny, we had to fight our way outta here, and now it's Zack's turn. Zack is a Martinez. He's *familia*. He doesn't belong running for refuge with strangers. No."

"So what was the answer?" everyone was thinking. Orlando went on.

"So I'm taking Zack up to LA with me and Manny," Orlando continued, answering the question. "He can be a roadie for the band for now. We'll work him so hard he won't have the time or energy to get in trouble." Orlando winked at his brother. "I'll take care of him, Pop, like I did with Manny. Remember him running wild in the *barrio* when I took over? I got him out of there, and now he's doing great."

Ernesto was surprised at how well Felix Martinez took the news. He seemed to be relieved. "Hey, Orlando," he piped up. "You may be right, yeah. The kid needs a change of scenery."

"And it's not like we won't come down plenty times and have some of Ma's cooking," Orlando declared. "Me and Manny and

Zack, we'll be around a lot. At Christmas time, you guys get to meet my chick— Marcella Delgado. And then in the summer, we'll be at Our Lady of Guadalupe Church. That's the old stomping grounds where the Martinez clan gets blessed and hitched. Right, Pop?"

Linda Martinez let out a little squeal of delight. "Orlando! Are you serious? You are getting married?"

"That's right, Mama," Orlando confirmed. "And then pretty soon there'll be *muchachas* and *muchachos* running around. You'll be good with them, Pop, like you were with us. You can take 'em hiking and fishing and play ball with them—the boys anyway. Maybe the girls too!"

Ernesto watched it all with admiration and wonderment. Orlando had righted a terrible situation. Orlando and Zack were hugging their parents and Naomi, and they laughed and shoved each other. The tears running down Mrs. Martinez's face were now tears of joy. Ernesto drew close to Naomi and whispered, "Orlando is something else. What a guy!"

The Martinez house still rang with laughter and noisy talk when Ernesto and Naomi went outside in the darkness to say goodnight.

"Babe," Ernesto declared, "next Friday, we'll go to the beach and barbecue. We'll do what we were gonna do tonight."

"You're on," Naomi agreed, "and it'll be even more wonderful."

Ernesto got home before ten o'clock. Both of his parents were in the living room, and they looked at him nervously when he came in.

"Everything okay with the Martinezes?" Luis Sandoval asked.

"Yeah," Ernesto replied, "Orlando came down from LA and straightened things out. Zack's gonna stay with him and Manny up there for a while. Orlando will take good care of Zack."

"Is Felix okay with that?" Dad asked warily.

"Yeah, Dad," Ernesto answered. "I think he realized he went too far with Zack. I think he got really scared that he'd driven the kid off. Mr. Martinez got worried that Zack was gonna be a loose cannon, and he'd fall in with anybody who'd have him. It happened with Manny. He was on the streets, getting into drugs, and Orlando rescued him too. Orlando is gonna make Zack a roadie, and he'll be too busy to get into trouble. I think their dad was grateful to Orlando for taking the kid. As nuts as he gets sometimes, Mr. Martinez does love his kids. If anything happened to any one of them I think it'd be over for him."

"I think you're right, Ernie," Dad agreed. "Felix loves his kids, but he just can't let go of his control."

Katalina appeared in the doorway in her pajamas. "It's not fair," she announced in a strident voice.

"Sweetheart," Mom told her, "you should be in bed. What are you doing out here, and what isn't fair?"

"That I can't invite the whole Lopez family to come and eat dinner with us," Katalina explained. "Andrea says all they eat is greasy old hamburgers and stuff. They eat those hard little lumps of chicken that aren't really chicken. I don't know what they are. They come in boxes and they taste horrible. I don't think it's fair that they can't all come over and eat with us one time."

Luis Sandoval looked at his wife, his eyebrows going up quizzically. "Well . . ." he said.

"Mom, that salmon you made was so good," Katalina continued. "If the Lopez family could come over some Sunday and have that—Andrea and Sarah and their dad and Cruz, too. I mean they'd be so happy . . ."

"Luis," Maria Sandoval said very softly, hoping Katalina wouldn't hear, "Cruz has a shaved head and all those tattoos."

"Mom!" Katalina cried, hearing every whispered word. "That quarterback for the Bengals that Daddy likes so much, he has a shaved head too. I mean, it's not fair. It's like being . . . prejudicial . . . or prejudiced. Why can't I invite my best friend in the whole world and her family over just one time for Sunday dinner?"

Luis Sandoval grinned ruefully at his wife. "It's happening already, *querida*. Our sweet little daughter is changing and we must change," he sighed.

Katalina's face lit up. "You mean I can? I can ask Andrea and her whole family over for Sunday dinner?"

"I guess so," Mom relented.

Katalina rushed over and hugged her mother and father. "Oh, Andrea'll be so excited. She told me nobody *ever* had her family over for dinner. Oh, she's gonna be so happy!" Katalina turned and raced back to her bedroom.

"She's calling Andrea right now, I'm sure" Luis Sandoval commented.

Maria Sandoval looked at her husband then and asked, "You don't think your mother will be shocked, do you?"

"By Cruz?" Dad asked.

"Yes, the shaved head, the tattoos. He wears earrings too, and I think there's a piercing in his . . . chin," Mom explained, her expression unhappy.

"Mama's pretty cool," Dad responded. "I took her shopping the other day, and we stopped at a jewelry counter downtown. The girl who waited on us had a nose ring and something in her tongue. She had a funny swatch of purple in her hair too. Mama wanted a little charm for a bracelet. Well, she just went on asking about the charms as if she didn't even notice the clerk was—"

"Freaky," Mom completed the sentence.

At school on Monday, Bianca Marquez sat next to Ernesto in AP History. "Would you have a few minutes at lunch? I'd like you to go over the rise of the Republican

Party with me. I get Hamilton's Federalists, but the Republicans . . ."

"You bet, Bianca," Ernesto said. "I need to go over that stuff too. We can help each other. We'll hit the machines and get something for lunch. Then we'll sneak off to a quiet place."

Mr. Bustos had not come into the room yet. Rod Garcia leaned back and looked Ernesto right in the eye. "You look confused, man," Garcia told him. "The class too hard for you? I heard you were busy trying to help the Martinez family with their wild son. Maybe you need to focus more on the class. This is hard stuff. You're playing with the big boys now."

"Don't worry about me, dude," Ernesto replied calmly. "I'll work it out." He figured if he didn't react with anger, Garcia would eventually get tired of baiting him.

Quino Bustos came striding into the room then, and soon a lively discussion was underway. "The rather bloody French Revolution was stirring the world," the teacher intoned. "At the same time, the Americans were building their own society in a much different way. How did our political leaders react to the violence in France?"

Bianca raised her hand nervously. Ernesto admired her for forcing herself out of her shy shell and trying to participate. He knew when he first met her that she was painfully shy. He thought it was courageous of her to be the first one to answer in class today.

"Yes, Bianca?" Mr. Bustos nodded toward her.

"Well, from what I read," the girl began, "the Americans didn't like the French Revolution at all. I mean, the way they were chopping heads off and . . . I mean, ours wasn't like that."

"Ah!" Mr. Bustos asked. "How did our friend Thomas Jefferson feel about the French Revolution?"

"I think he didn't like the violent part," Bianca answered.

Rod Garcia eagerly raised his hand.

Ernesto's heart sank. Poor Bianca had tried so hard, and she had said the wrong thing. Now Garcia was eager to show her up.

"Yes, Rod?" Mr. Bustos said.

"Jefferson was a big admirer of the French Revolution," Rod Garcia crowed. "He called it a victory over despotism. He wasn't bothered by the shedding of blood if that's what it took to set things right over there."

"Exactly," Mr. Bustos confirmed, smiling at Garcia. "The news of the Reign of Terror in France had spread to the United States. Americans knew of the many executions by the drastic method of the guillotine. Yet Jefferson and the Jeffersonians stood with the forces that opposed the monarchy in France. And how then did Mr. Hamilton stand on this issue?"

When Ernesto raised his hand, Rod Garcia snickered. He thought Ernesto would drop the ball too. In Rod's mind, Ernesto Sandoval was a stupid jerk. He was in way over his head, not only as senior class president but in this college-level class. "Edmund Burke wrote a strong condemnation of the French Revolution," Ernesto answered. "And the Hamiltonians showed profound disgust at the extremes of the Reign of Terror."

"Very true, Ernesto," Mr. Bustos said with pleasure.

Ernesto was glad he had gained the teacher's respect, but he was still feeling bad about Bianca. She'd stuck her neck out of the bunker and got a bullet for her trouble.

After class, Ernesto led the way to the vending machines. He wanted to get the girl's mind off her error. "I don't know about you, Bianca," he declared, "but I'm starved." Ernesto knew what it was like to make a mistake in front of the whole class. You kept reliving it and suffering the embarrassment over and over.

"I'm not very hungry," Bianca responded. "I don't need any more calories either."

Ernesto usually brought his own lunch. But with all the excitement over at the Martinez house, he forgot to pack anything. Now he bought a chicken salad sandwich from the machine, and Bianca just bought soda, a diet soda.

When they sat down, Bianca remarked, "I've always been an overachiever. I mean, I study real hard, but I'm not as smart as my mom. She teaches at the community college."

"My dad teaches here at Chavez," Ernesto replied. "But he teaches a couple evening classes at the college too."

"I felt like such a fool today," Bianca said sadly. "I mean, everybody must be wondering what a dummy like me is doing in an advanced placement class."

"Bianca, we all do stuff like that at one time or another," he reasoned. "I remember one time in middle school. We were studying about the different ethnic groups, and one of them was the Alpines. Our teacher was very proud to be part of this ethnic group. So he went on and on that this was one of the three great races of Europe. They had moderate stature and nice sort of dark complexion."

Ernesto flashed a big smile. He was trying to show her his goof was no big thing. "Well, the next day, the teacher asks me to describe the Alpines. I go, 'Those big mountains in Switzerland.' I'd confused the word with the Alps, and the whole class broke out laughing. I was kind of a skinny, wimpy kid in those days, and a lot of the guys didn't like me anyway. Even my teacher kinda had it in for me after that, but I survived. Don't sweat it, Bianca."

As Ernesto was eating his chicken salad sandwich, he watched the girl sipping her diet soda. "You sure you don't want to get something to eat, Bianca? A diet soda isn't enough for lunch."

"No, no, I'm fine," Bianca insisted. "I have issues with my weight. My mother and I both put on weight easily, and then it's a bear to take off. Mom is a fanatic

115

about exercise and eating mostly salads. She always skips lunch. She used to wear size twelve, but now that she's been dieting and running, she's down to a size two. She looks so great. My grandma's a size twelve, and she looks so fat that Mom's embarrassed to go anywhere with her."

"No offense, Bianca," Ernesto objected, "but you look awfully thin, like you're a size zero or something."

"Oh no, I need to lose five pounds," Bianca countered.

Ernesto loved the way Naomi Martinez looked. He figured she was size 6, but whatever she was, she looked fabulous. To Ernesto, Naomi always looked great in her clothes, no matter what she wore. Ernesto loved the healthy glow to her face. He loved how she dug into a good meal, enjoying every bite and not worrying about calories. Ernesto's mother was closing in on forty, and she was the same way. His mom and his girl both had lovely, healthy figures, and they didn't stress about every pound.

There was something about Bianca's thinness, though, that disturbed Ernesto very much.

Ernesto and Bianca spent about thirty minutes going over the rise of the Republican Party. At the end of the study period, Bianca said she'd never fully understood it before this. Now she did. "Maybe I won't make a fool of myself again when we get to this stuff," she sighed. She looked pained again as she remembered her gaffe.

"Bianca, forget what happened today," Ernesto ordered.

"Well," she replied, "the Republican Party was as clear as mud to me until you went over it, Ernie. Now I'm good."

"Great. And any time you need some study time, even after school when I'm home, we can work on the computer together. That's the beauty of that technology, Bianca," Ernesto said.

"Thanks so much, Ernie. You're awfully nice," Bianca told him as she gathered her books and notes.

"*Por nada*," Ernesto responded. "And one more thing, Bianca. Don't lose that five pounds. Trust me. I'm a guy. I *know* what a girl is supposed to look like. I'm a guy and I know—"

Bianca laughed. It was good to see her laugh. It didn't happen too often from what Ernesto saw.

After school that day, Ernesto went over to the new coffee shop across the street with Naomi. He told her all about Bianca Marquez.

"It's good that you're helping her, Ernie," Naomi told him. "She seems kinda troubled. I think she's got problems at home."

"Yeah, I got that," Ernesto confirmed. "She's so thin. It's almost like it's dangerous, you know?"

"I think she's right on the edge of being anorexic, Ernie," Naomi said. "I've talked to her about it. She says her mom is real thin too. I read in a psychology site online that when people kinda lose control of their lives, they take control of their diets. But they do it in a really crazy way 'cause that gives them the sense that they're at least on top of things. I could never do that. I mean, I try to eat healthy and stuff, but I love a good meal."

"Me too," Ernesto agreed.

When the frappés came, Ernesto asked Naomi how things were going in the Martinez house.

"It wasn't bad at all once Orlando left with Zack," Naomi replied, taking a sip of her drink. "We had our nice friendly good-byes and stuff. Mom cried, of course, but not the bitter tears she'd been crying. I think she's relieved. The tension between Zack and Dad isn't going on anymore in the house."

The girl's face took on a pensive look. "I hope Dad starts paying more attention to Mom now," Naomi went on. "He needs to take Mom out to dinner and do fun stuff with her. Mom hasn't gotten a lot of that over the years. Now that the boys are all out of the house, maybe there'll be time for my parents."

"Yeah," Ernesto agreed, "they need to get that in now. It won't be long before Orlando gets married, and the grandkids start coming. That'll be a whole other distraction. I'm anxious to meet Orlando's fiancée. He said she sings with the Oscar Perez band with him. I bet she's hot. Orlando is such a hunk himself. He'd have to pick a hot chick. Have you met the girl, Naomi?"

"I haven't, no," Naomi responded, shaking her head. "I've never seen her singing with the band either. Orlando's been keeping her a big secret. I can't wait to meet her. I bet she's nice. I want to be really friendly with her 'cuz that's the closest I'm going to get to having sisters."

"Well, Katalina and Juanita consider you a sister, Naomi," Ernesto told her, chuckling. "So there's that too."

Naomi was laughing when Ernesto's phone rang.

"Hi, Mom," Ernesto said. Then the pleasant expression on his face changed quickly. He looked concerned. "When? . . . Just now? . . .

Is she conscious, Mom? . . . Oh man," he groaned. "I'll be right home. I'll drop Naomi home and then I'll be there, Mom." He put down the phone. "My *abuela*," he explained. "She fell, and she can't get up. Mom thinks she maybe broke a hip."

Naomi reached over and put her hand over Ernesto's. His father's widowed mother, Lena Sandoval, had been living with the family now for almost a year. Katalina and Juanita totally loved her. *Abuela* helped them with their homework every day. She was a playmate and a tutor for the girls. And she was a big help to Mom, now that she had a newborn baby to care for.

"I'm so sorry, Ernie. Is there anything I can do?" Naomi asked.

"No, thanks. They've called nine-nine-one," Ernesto answered, getting up and leaving most of his frappé. Ernesto and Naomi rushed to his Volvo and headed toward Naomi's house. As he dropped Naomi in her driveway, Ernesto told her, "I'll text you later, babe."

CHAPTER SEVEN

By the time Ernesto reached the Sandoval house on Wren Street, the paramedics were in the driveway. Ernesto parked and ran to the gurney where his *abuela* lay. He glanced at the frail little figure, and he turned numb.

Katalina and Juanita were with Mom, and the girls were crying.

"She'll be okay," Mom was saying, over and over. "Everything will be fine. *Abuela* will be home in no time."

Ernesto glanced at his father. Ernesto remembered when he was a small boy and Dad learned that his father had died. The grandfather Ernesto was named after— *Abuelo* Luis Ernesto—had died suddenly.

Ernesto remembered his father leaning over, shaking with sobs.

Ernesto leaned over the gurney and kissed his *abuela*. "Does it hurt much?" he asked her softly.

"Just a little," she responded, managing a smile. "It was so dumb of me. I didn't see Calico lying there in the middle of the hall. I just tripped over her. It was my own fault."

Ernesto had seen Calico lying underfoot a hundred times. Cats did that. Younger people just stumbled a little or inadvertently kicked the cat. But *Abuela* was a frail, older person, and she could easily lose her balance.

Maria Sandoval came to Ernesto and spoke hurriedly. "I'm riding in the ambulance with Mama. Your father is following in our car. You've got to see after the girls and little Alfredo. I'll be home as soon as I can."

"Okay, Mom. I'll be praying," Ernesto promised.

Ernesto watched the ambulance back from the driveway, turning onto Tremayne, followed by the family minivan.

Katalina huddled against Ernesto and groaned. "Poor *Abuela*. I bet she's scared riding in the ambulance. I hope she didn't break her hip. Maybe it's just bruised."

Ernesto put his arm around his little sister's shoulders and gave her a hug. "It'll be okay," he consoled. "Hey, is Alfredo sleeping?"

"Yeah, Juanita is with him," Katalina answered. "Oh, Ernie, this is so awful. Why did Calico do such a thing? I stumble over Calico all the time. She's a bad cat. She doesn't have to lay there where people walk!"

"She's a cat," Ernesto stated flatly. "She doesn't know she's in the way. She can't figure things out. She plops down wherever she wants."

Brother and sister turned to walk into the house.

"*Abuela* will be all right, won't she?" Katalina asked. "Even if she broke her hip, the doctors can fix it, can't they?" A few days ago, Ernesto thought, Katalina was demanding that the Lopez family be invited to Sunday dinner. She seemed so much older then than she did now. Now, in her fear for her beloved grandmother, she was a very little girl again.

"Yeah, Kat," Ernesto assured her, "even if her hip is broken, they can put a pin in. She's going to be laid up for a few weeks. And she'll need to use a walker when she comes home, at least for a while. But then she'll be fine with a cane."

"Do you think it hurts her a lot, Ernie?" Katalina asked, her eyes wide.

"They'll give her medicine for the pain," Ernesto said.

"Ernie, you know how *Abuela* likes to run to the store and stuff," Katalina commented. "She won't like having to use an old walker. She's gonna be so sad."

"Kat, *Abuela* is in her seventies," he explained. "She'll just have to walk a little

125

slower while her hip heals. And we'll all have to help her."

"I'll check the house for anything that could make her fall again," Katalina declared.

"Good girl!" Ernesto said. He heard a sound then. He'd heard it before, of course. But when Mom was home or even Dad, he didn't pay much attention to it. Little Alfredo was crying. Maybe he was hungry. Mom had left a bottle of formula.

"Ernie!" Juanita yelled from their parents' bedroom where Alfredo slept. "Alfredo smells bad."

Ernesto slowed. Maybe Juanita made a mistake, he thought. All babies smell a little funny. Maybe he spit up some milk or something. Ernesto was not anxious to go into the bedroom. He was wondering how soon Mom and Dad would be home. If *Abuela* did break her hip, it would take time to do the x-rays and then assign her a room. The operation to repair her hip would probably be tomorrow. Mom and Dad would want to be there for the operation. But they'd be home tonight, in a few hours.

"Alfredo smells really awful," Juanita announced in a strident voice. Ernesto was about to go into the bedroom and man up to changing his brother's diaper. Then the doorbell rang. Ernesto went to the door and saw Linda Martinez and Naomi. Mrs. Martinez came in first, followed by Naomi.

"You poor dear," Mrs. Martinez cried. "Naomi told me what happened. Your grandmother broke her hip, they think? Are your parents at the hospital with her? And here you are with your sisters and the baby. We had to come over."

"Uh . . . won't your husband mind?" Ernesto asked, though he was filled with relief.

"His cousin Monte is over and they're watching a basketball game," Linda Martinez explained. "They won't even know we're gone. I left plenty of chips and salsa."

"Ernie," Juanita yelled, "Alfredo needs changing right now!"

Naomi and her mother smiled, and they both disappeared into the bedroom. "Poor little baby!" Linda Martinez was cooing. "In all the excitement, they forgot about you. You want a nice clean didee, and we have one coming up."

"I got the baby wipes right here," Naomi said.

Reassuring sounds of baby giggles and female laughter came from the bedroom. Finally, Mrs. Martinez announced, "There now. That's better, isn't it, Alfredo? What a good baby you are. What a go-o-o-od little baby. Yes, you are!"

"Wow!" Ernesto exclaimed. "Thanks for coming over. I never expected . . . I mean, I could've done it. But oh man, it was so good of you to come over."

Most other times that Ernesto saw Linda Martinez, she was in distress of some sort. She was crying, worried, or standing in the corner of the room in the Martinez house, trembling at the turmoil. Now she looked calm and pretty as she walked over to Ernesto and caressed his cheek.

"Ernesto," she said softly, "how many times have you been there for us?"

In the days that followed, Lena Sandoval's broken hip was repaired, and she began physical therapy. All the members of the family helped her: her daughters, Magda and Hortencia, and her sons, Arturo and Luis and their wives. Conchita Ibarra and Linda Martinez visited her often in rehab. They cheered her on as she increased the number of steps she took in her walker every day.

Three weeks later, *Abuela* Lena returned to the little house on Wren Street. Her daughter Magda had insisted that her mother should return to her home permanently. "This is no place for Mama," Magda griped. "Two little girls, a baby, a cat. It's too much for an old lady."

Abuela Lena laughed and replied, "Magda, Magda! It is so boring in your house. I love the *niñas* and *niños*. They make me feel young again."

"We love having your mom here," Maria Sandoval told Magda. "And she does seem so happy. She's bonded with Katalina and Juanita. And I think little Alfredo is the most peaceful in her arms.

Magda glared at her mother. "You were always stubborn, Mama," she scolded.

"Yes," *Abuela* Lena replied, giggling.

When Katalina and Juanita came home from school, they screamed in delight to see their grandmother. Right away the homework club was underway. *Abuela* Lena was getting around better and better in her walker. And the girls were attentive to all obstacles. The physical therapist said she was close to needing only a cane.

Ernesto was also very happy to have his grandmother home. She was so easy to get along with. She wasn't critical of anything or anybody. But a problem was looming on the horizon: Ernesto's mother's parents were coming for a visit. Eva Vasquez, Luis

Sandoval's mother-in-law, had learned of the grandmother's broken hip. She'd been texting dire messages that taking care of *Abuela* would be too much of an added burden for her daughter. Her mother-in-law must go to a nursing home at once, she declared.

Eva Vasquez always found something in the Sandoval house to be unhappy about. Ernesto did not mind *Abuelo* Alfredo, his mom's dad. He was a nice, congenial man. Ever since little Alfredo had been named after him, he was always visited in an even better mood. He was so proud of his little namesake. Ernesto often wished his grandmother would stay home and let grandfather come alone.

At school, Ernesto had another worry: whom the senior class would choose as the king and queen of the homecoming events.

Rod Garcia was already bitter about losing the senior class presidency to Ernesto. Now he was determined that his girlfriend,

Lisa Castillo, would be homecoming queen. Rod also figured that, since he lost the senior class presidency, he had the right to be chosen king. It would be fair recognition of all the work he had done in the school's clubs. Rod had been relentlessly active in extracurricular activities. But to him, the clubs were only a way to assure himself the senior class presidency. Rod had run clubs that he had no interest in, like the ecology club. He'd thought that all that boring drudgery should get him something. When Ernesto became senior class president, Rod felt bitter and cheated. Being the homecoming king, alongside Lisa as the queen, seemed like a chance to at least partially set things right.

Ernesto could have said a few things to Rod, but Rod hated him enough already. So Ernesto did *not* tell him what a lot of the students knew. Everybody saw through Rod's strategy. He was totally unenthusiastic during many of the activities he led. So now Rod Garcia was less popular than ever. Not many students, Ernesto figured, would vote for him or Lisa Castillo. Ernesto doubted either one of the couple would win the prize, and he dreaded a fresh barrage of Rod's fury. Basically, Ernesto would have liked to see the whole homecoming king and queen idea dumped.

"Garcia thinks he's got homecoming king coming to him," Ernesto told his friends at lunch. "And he thinks his girlfriend will get to be queen."

Abel Ruiz shrugged his shoulders. "Lots of girls prettier and lots nicer than Lisa Castillo, like Naomi and Carmen."

"Leave me out of it, I beg you," Naomi groaned. "I've got plenty enough drama in my life now. I don't even like the idea of kings and queens. The thought of a bunch of girls clawing and scratching for the honor makes me sick."

Carmen Ibarra laughed. "They'd never pick me. I've got too big a mouth. I've made a lotta enemies. Having my pop a city councilman doesn't help either. Every time somebody busts an alignment on a pot hole they yell at me."

Carmen's tone turned serious then. "You know who'd be a good choice? She's nice and pretty and she needs an ego boost too."

"Who?" Ernesto asked, as he finished his pear.

"Bianca Marquez," Carmen declared. "She's kinda down on herself, and she's slipping into anorexia. Still, she's so statuesque and pretty."

"Yeah," Naomi commented, "she'd be good. Another one would be Yvette Ozono. She's had so much tragedy in her life. Yet she's come from almost nothing to be an excellent student. She's gorgeous with that curly black hair and those big eyes."

"Yeah," Carmen agreed. "I'd love to see Yvette get it. She's really inspirational. Everybody likes her a lot."

"There are so many nice girls," Abel remarked. "Lisa Castillo's stuck on herself, and being Garcia's chick doesn't help either."

"Next Friday afternoon," Ernesto declared, "we're gonna announce the three themes for the homecoming dance. The kids can vote on them. Some of the suggestions we got were awful. But Ms. Wilson and I whittled the list down to the three that came up most often. After that, the king and queen voting starts. Students have to put in their names, and Ms. Wilson checks if they're academically qualified. I could do without all this social junk. But," Ernesto announced, his face brightening, "I'm really jazzed about how many seniors are signing up for the tutoring program."

"What are the three themes, dude," Abel asked, "or is that classified?"

"Nope," Ernesto answered, rolling up his bag of after-lunch trash. " 'Vanishing Dawn,' that song getting all the play on YouTube. That came up a lot. Then the song that that new teen idol sings—'Purple Midnight.' It's not a very good song, but he's very popular now. Then the third one is that song from the Oscar Perez band, 'Estrellas fugaces.' I really like that one."

"Oh wow! That's the one Orlando sings," Naomi exclaimed. "Wouldn't it be amazing if that song was chosen for the theme? That would be just amazing."

Ernesto laughed. "Naomi, now you sound like Deprise Wilson. Everything is amazing to her. But the Perez song is the best, and it'd make a great theme."

"It'd be a natural for decorating the gym," Naomi remarked. "Shooting stars. Is that romantic or what?"

"We could just fill the gym ceiling with sparkling stars," Carmen suggested.

"Well, I hope it wins," Ernesto concluded. "I think the other two are kinda lame myself."

Ernesto lay back on the grass and looked up at the blue sky. Clouds were etched into the blue, but they were high cirrus clouds without the threat of rain. The weather was nice, and Ernesto was hoping for a good weekend.

He thought about Andres Lopez and his family, who were coming to the Sandoval house for Sunday dinner. Katalina and Juanita were really excited. They'd been promising their friends a Sunday dinner for a long time. But it had been put off when *Abuela* broke her hip.

"I don't know what Mom's gonna make for the Lopezes," Ernesto mused. "She hasn't said anything."

"She has nothing to worry about," Abel stated with a funny smile. Abel Ruiz had been making dinners for his friends and their families for almost a year now. Each one of them seemed more spectacular than the last. Though he was still in high school, he worked part-time as junior chef at the ritzy restaurant—the Sting Ray. And he had a scholarship for culinary school waiting for him as soon as he graduated. His dream in life was to become a chef and one day to open his own restaurant. "Yeah, I got something good planned, Ernie," Abel assured his friend. "Your mom and I got it all figured out."

"Wow!" Ernesto exclaimed. "You're awesome, dude."

Mentally, Ernesto breathed a sigh of relief. *Abuela* Lena was doing better each day with her walking, but she still needed help. Mom was working on her books again, and she had plenty to do. She didn't need to worry about Sunday dinner. Abel's help was a big plus.

"Mom thinks you're a genius, Abel," Ernesto announced. "For a guy your age to be able to turn out the meals you make, it's incredible. Your mom must be really proud of you."

Abel grimaced. "Tomás is still the star in the family, Ernie," Abel protested. "If I won the Nobel Peace Prize, I don't think I could knock my big brother off his pedestal. Me and Penelope are forever condemned to be the less magnificent siblings."

"Well, we sure appreciate what you're doing, Abel," Ernesto said.

"Look, dude," Abel responded, "I'll never forget the guy who got me to follow my dream in the first place. I was just drifting, man. Then you told me everybody needs to find his passion, his dream. You got me going."

Ernesto had inspired Abel to discover his secret talent for cooking, and Abel took it from there. Before then, Abel had become convinced that his mother was right. He considered himself a sort of a loser like his father, somebody who couldn't excel at anything. He was always a good kid but nobody special, he thought. Abel's cooking changed all that. He blossomed. He even got some respect from his parents, and he felt like a man. And feeling like a man was the most important thing.

"Your mom and grandma gonna be cool with Cruz?" Abel asked. "The dude takes some getting used to."

"Yeah, *Abuela*'s pretty cool," Ernesto answered. "She sees the low riders in the neighborhood, and she just laughs. I'm more worried about my mom. Mom doesn't know what to make of Cruz. Guys with shaved heads and tattoos, you know. It'd be good if he was more like us, but he's not."

Ernesto was staring at the sky, hands clasped behind his head. "And my little sisters just love his sisters. Kat's best friend in school is Andrea. And Kat's been pleading with Mom to have the family over for dinner. I guess, from what Kat says anyway, that their dad doesn't do much cooking. On his way home from work, he stops at the fast-food place. So it's always pizza or hamburgers, stuff like that."

"They've been struggling all right," Abel remarked. "When Cruz's mom was alive and their dad was working, they had to be careful about money, but life was okay. Mrs. Lopez made nice meals for the kids, healthy meals. But you know how it goes. When you take the mom out of the home, something really awful happens. I think moms are sorta like the heart of a family."

"Yeah," Ernesto agreed. He didn't even want to think of what life would be like in their house without Mom. The thought was so terrible that he pushed it swiftly from his mind. He didn't let it to linger for a second. "Sunday dinner at our house'll be a big treat for them," Ernesto added. "Especially for the girls, and Cruz too. He was really close to his mom, and he misses her."

CHAPTER EIGHT

That Sunday, Abel Ruiz showed up at the Sandoval house about an hour before any of the guests arrived.

"This is an entrée we've introduced at the Sting Ray," Abel explained. "And it's really going over big, Mrs. Sandoval. Korean barbecued beef. I've already marinated it, and it's ready for the skillet. Got the green onions all chopped. Some chopped garlic, pepper, soy sauce, and we're good to go."

"Oh my, the sirloin looks so good," Maria Sandoval sighed. Abel had told her what he needed, and she bought everything. Everything seemed to be ready.

"Then we got the honey lime fruit salad, lots of cut-up fresh fruit, cantaloupe, watermelon," Abel continued. "And for dessert, key lime pie."

"They are so lucky to have you down at the Sting Ray, Abel," Mom commented. "And at home!" She turned to Ernesto. "Honey," she kidded him, "how come all you can make are peanut butter and jelly sandwiches?"

Ernesto laughed. "The luck of the draw, Mom," he responded.

The Sandovals urged Abel to stay for dinner and take a bow for his wonderful meal. But he didn't want to do that. He had to go to work at the Sting Ray that afternoon anyway.

"*Adios!*" Abel cried, slipping out the back door of the Sandoval house. At about the same time, a well-worn station wagon creaked and wheezed its way into the driveway. Mr. Lopez, Cruz, and the two Lopez girls got out. They were all dressed nicely, even Cruz. They had all made an effort to look as presentable as their clothes closet allowed.

"They're here!" Katalina cried, running to the front door. Ernesto noticed that Mr. Lopez wore a threadbare but decent suit. Cruz, usually clad in a T-shirt with disturbing messages, wore a nice pair of slacks and a faded green polo shirt. The little girls had managed to find cute, colorful tops to go with their skinny jeans. Ernesto was deeply touched by how this family was trying to present themselves in as best light as possible.

Maria Sandoval swung the front door open wide. "Come on in Mr. Lopez, Cruz, Andrea, and Sarah." she greeted. "You all look so nice."

"It was so kind of you to invite us to your home, Mrs. Sandoval," Mr. Lopez said shyly. "My daughters have told me so many wonderful things about your girls and your family."

Ernesto figured this was probably the first time anybody in the *barrio* had invited the Lopez family to Sunday dinner. Andrea and Sarah Lopez had already been in the

Sandoval house. They had had a few play dates with Katalina and Juanita. Ernesto's mother had picked them up from school with her own girls. When it was time to go, Mom delivered them home in the early evening. But Mr. Lopez and Cruz had never been inside the house.

"Your house is very beautiful," Mr. Lopez observed.

"Thank you," Luis Sandoval said. He introduced the Lopez family to his mother. Then they all sat down to eat. Cruz was wide-eyed as Mom brought the food to the table. The beef was presented on a bed of fried rice and garnished with chopped scallions. The side dish was a luscious-looking salad.

"What's this?" Andrea asked, taking a taste of the Korean barbecued beef. "It's sooo good."

"Korean barbecued beef, honey," Mom responded. "I must confess that I didn't make it. We have a good friend, Abel Ruiz. He's an assistant chef at a fine restaurant, and he cooked this meal for us."

Cruz's face lit up. "I *know* Abel. He's cool," he remarked.

Sarah took a forkful of the honey lime fruit salad. "Oh, I love everything!" she cried.

"The children don't get enough fruits and vegetables," Mr. Lopez commented sadly. "Not enough homemade food. My wife, she made wonderful dinners. She could make something out of almost nothing."

"I remember my health teacher in middle school was always after us to eat salads and stuff," Cruz recalled. "But every salad I ever ate was so lame. But this stuff is really good. I'm gonna ask Abel how he makes it. Maybe I could make this stuff for us sometimes."

"What a good idea," Mom agreed. "So, Cruz, how are your classes at the community college going?"

"Okay," Cruz replied, finishing a mouthful of beef. "I'm getting the hang of the electrical stuff. Beto and me can really make good kitchen cabinets and stuff like that. Our teacher said we should be able to get some good jobs when we're finished." Cruz turned to Ernesto's father and said, "You gave us a good steer, Mr. Sandoval. I don't know what we'd be doing now if we hadn't gone into college. Maybe getting arrested."

After the entrée and salad was finished, the group relaxed at the table and chatted a while. The aroma of percolating coffee wafted from the kitchen. Then Maria Sandoval brought out the key lime pie, cut it, and passed out the slices.

Ernesto thought Andrea and Sarah's eyes would pop out of their heads. Cruz tasted the pie. "Wow!" he exclaimed. "This is good. It sure doesn't taste like the pie they sell in the cardboard boxes."

"I'll say," Andrea added.

"It's homemade," *Abuela* Lena stated solemnly. "Homemade is always better."

After dessert and more conversation, the Lopezes were ready to go home. At the door, they thanked the Sandovals profusely.

In fact, Ernesto thought his parents looked embarrassed. Nobody had ever been so grateful for being invited to a Sunday dinner at the Sandoval house. The Lopez family left, and the door closed after them.

Maria Sandoval turned to her daughter with a look of shame on her face. "Oh, Katalina," Mom said, "I almost didn't let them come! What kind of person am I? They were all so grateful, I feel like a mean little person."

Mom and the girls went toward the kitchen, as Ernesto and Dad cleared the table. "When Mrs. Lopez died," Mom continued, "we all went to the funeral. Since then, you, Ernie, and you girls, have stayed in touch. But Luis and I haven't reached out to that poor motherless family. We should have had them over months ago."

Mom took the apron hanging on the back of the kitchen door. She spoke as she put it on. "But that boy, Cruz, he seemed so strange. Now that I've met him, he seems like just a kid desperately trying to fit in. Once you get past the tattoos and the shaved head, he's just a little boy. He's just someone who lost his mother too soon. And they were all trying so hard to be presentable."

"It was good we had them over," Luis Sandoval declared. "People like that need to feel that they're part of community, not outcasts. We'll have them over again real soon."

All during the next week, Ernesto geared up for the senior class meeting. When it was just hours away on Friday, Ernesto and Deprise Wilson chatted in her office.

"We have three good names submitted for the theme," Ms. Wilson remarked. "But one of the names is just amazing. It just jumps out at me. It's lovely, and it's so easy to decorate for. I wonder if you agree with me, Ernie? This one song seems to stand out above the other two—"

Ernesto smiled and finished Ms. Wilson's thought. " 'Estrellas fugaces.'"

"Ernie!" the young teacher squealed. "That's it! It just sends chills up my spine, it's so beautiful. I've heard it on YouTube, and it's on my iPhone. I can't get enough of it. It has so much heart, and the young man who sings it is just amazing."

"That's Orlando Martinez," Ernesto told her. "He's Naomi Martinez's brother. You know her. She's a senior."

Deprise Wilson's already large eyes turned into dinner plates. "Oh my goodness! Naomi is such a darling girl. I had no idea she had a brother in the music business. Why, the young man is famous!"

"Well, he's getting there anyway," Ernesto granted. "Now when you get a lot of play online, you're halfway there. It's not like in the old days. Kids used to start in little clubs and hope somebody would see them. They'd hope that somebody important enough to get them started would spot them. Now the artists go right to the people. If they're good, they take off like rockets."

"What a wonderful, exciting world we live in," Deprise Wilson commented, her eyes glowing.

At the senior class meeting, Deprise Wilson took her usual place in the back of the auditorium. Ernesto and the other senior class officers took the stage. Ernesto was consoled to see many of his friends already there. But Rod Garcia, Clay Aguirre, and their friends were there too, filling up the front seats. They'd arrived extra early to make sure that they'd be up front.

Ernesto's legs felt a little unsteady. Seeing Rod and Clay glaring at him had that effect. Then Ernesto remembered his father's tip. He looked at Naomi, Abel, Carmen, and his other friends.

The last few students entered and took their seats. Ernesto rose and strode to the podium.

"First off," he began, "we're going to announce the three songs submitted for the homecoming theme. All the other suggestions were good too. But Ms. Wilson whittled the list down to the three that came up most often. We've printed the three winners on ballots, and you can get them in your homerooms and vote."

Ernesto read the three suggested song names. When he got to "Estrellas fugaces," the auditorium buzzed with excitement. The song clearly resonated with a lot of the seniors. Ernesto wasn't sure how much of it was due to the big play the song was getting online. Maybe the girls just liked watching the handsome Orlando Martinez singing the song in his passionate tenor.

But Rod Garcia didn't look happy. He raised his hand with a sour look on his face. Ernesto dreaded whatever annoying objections he must now have. "Yeah, Rod," Ernesto sighed, recognizing him.

"You know," Rod Garcia began, "I don't know how many of us feel the way I do. But it irks me to think we'd pick a song that's in Spanish and not English. Yeah, we all mostly come from Hispanic backgrounds. But this is the United States of America, and we're American kids. I say our homecoming theme should be a song in English."

Rod turned to glance back at the audience. Perhaps he thought he would have more support for his idea. But no one said anything.

"This isn't Mexico," he went on, swinging his head back toward the stage. "Yeah, a lot of the old people in the *barrio* rattle off in Spanish all the time. Or maybe somebody who just came over the border doesn't speak English yet. But we should be beyond that. We're second- and third-generation Americans. We don't need a Spanish song for the homecoming events."

The light smattering of applause came mainly from Clay Aguirre, Lisa Castillo, and their little clique. Rod sat down, looking very pleased with himself.

Carmen's hand shot up. "You know what?" she noted. " 'Estrellas' is a beautiful song with great music. There've been popular songs in German, French, Spanish. If they're good, they take off. It's no big deal. We can all vote, right? We got a democracy going here, guys, so let's go for it." The girl sat down.

"Yeah," Abel piped up, "music is like food. The best kind is a mix of everything. That's why American music is so good. We mix country, jazz, rock. And it comes from all kinds of countries. You name it."

The seniors broke out in applause for Carmen and Abel. But Rod Garcia refused to give up. He was back on his feet.

"I don't care what anybody says," he persisted. "I just resent that we're trying to pretend Spanish is better than English. That's a big problem anyway around here: people hanging onto their old language and flunking school and stuff." Rod glared with menace at Abel. "And I think it's stupid to compare music and food."

For Ernesto, this moment could make or break him as senior class president. He wanted to put down Rod Garcia, but that would have been a disaster. Most of the seniors didn't like or agree with Rod. But he was expressing his opinion, even if it went against the grain. Most of the kids respected that.

Ernesto spoke in a calm, measured voice. "Well, I want to thank Rod and Carmen and Abel for their spirited remarks. They are obviously heartfelt opinions. I want you all to speak up about things you care about. But let's remember that we're all loyal members of the Cesar Chavez senior class. Whatever is decided will get our support. We all want the best homecoming week ever."

The whole auditorium burst into applause. Ernesto thought he'd struck the right tone. He was relieved and happy, although he clearly saw the anger in Rod's eyes.

Ernesto went on to describe the procedures for nominating students for homecoming king and queen. Then he closed the meeting and exited the auditorium with Ms. Wilson.

Without comment, Ms. Wilson patted Ernesto on the arm, smiled, and bustled down the hallway. Ernesto headed for his Volvo with a spring in his step. The senior class meeting went even better than he'd hoped. Better still, tonight he was finally going to the beach for that long postponed barbecue. Abel and Claudia, Paul and Carmen, and, of course, Naomi would all be going.

When Ernie reached his Volvo, he noticed something new on the door. It was no big deal because the car was old and rusty in places. But somebody had keyed his old white Volvo. Someone had taken the trouble to scratch in a word, using a nail, a screwdriver, or some sharp object.

The five letters spelled—"creep."

Ernesto shrugged. He wasn't going to let this vandalism spoil his good feelings. He was still elated over the successful senior class meeting. He wasn't going to let a few scratches put a damper on tonight.

Ernesto got behind the wheel and turned the ignition key. Ernesto was trying to shrug off the incident. Still, it hurt that somebody would take the trouble to seek out his car and gouge out that mean-spirited word. He thought immediately of Rod Garcia or Clay Aguirre. But maybe somebody else hated him, somebody he didn't even know. Maybe some kid was sitting way in the back. Maybe somebody resented Ernesto for being a big shot or for some other reason.

Ernesto headed for the supermarket to pick up supplies for the beach party. Ernesto had promised to bring sodas, so he put some regular and diet into his cart. He also picked up orange juice for those who didn't want carbonated drinks. He loaded them in the Volvo, deliberately looking past the word "creep" on the front door. "Tomorrow," he thought, "I'll just paint over it. Another good reason to be driving a junker." Ernesto grinned wryly.

The other kids were bringing all the other supplies.

Ernesto picked up Naomi at her house at six. They were supposed to all meet at the beach at six thirty.

Naomi wore a bright red top and skinny jeans. Ernesto thought she looked incredible. He was always awed by how beautiful she was and still how nice she was. Most girls who looked like her could be stuck-up and impossible to please, Ernesto thought. For some strange reason, Naomi Martinez never caught on to how beautiful she really was.

"Ernie," Naomi said when she got in the car. "You were sooo good at the senior class meeting today. I was so proud of you! You didn't let Rod get to you with his ridiculous objections. Ernie, I was just holding my breath thinking you'd tell Rod Garcia to shut up, but you didn't. You actually treated him with respect, which he didn't deserve. You were a class act, Ernie. No wonder so many of us voted for you!"

"Thanks, Naomi," Ernesto responded. "That means a lot to hear you say that. I never know how I'm really coming across when I'm up there in front of the class."

"I can just see you in the courtroom, a brilliant and persuasive lawyer," Naomi predicted dramatically.

"Yeah, I hope," Ernesto chuckled. "I got a lot to get through before that happens. Law school's tough, and then there's passing the bar. Uncle Arturo said it's no snap."

"You can do it, Ernie," Naomi assured him. She snuggled up to his shoulder as he drove. "I think you could do anything you set your mind to doing."

"Except change Alfredo," Ernesto commented with a laugh.

"Oh, come on," Naomi chided. "You could have done that too, Ernie. But Mom and I thought we should come over and help. Mom really loves you, Ernie. You're some kind of a superhero to her. Of course, she's right. How am I going to argue with the truth?"

Ernesto smiled. "Babe, you make me feel ten feet tall," he responded. Then he asked, "Have you heard from Zack since he's up there in LA with your brothers?"

"Yeah, he calls Mom every day," Naomi answered. "He sometimes talks to Dad too. He tells us how hard he's working. Orlando has Zack on a short leash. Oh, Orlando is a slave driver, and he can't go anywhere or do anything he wants to do. He says Orlando is worse than Dad, and that makes Dad happy, of course. Pop's delighted that somebody as tough as him is keeping Zack out of trouble."

"Well, I'm glad it's working out, babe," Ernesto commented. Then he added, "You know, some joker keyed my car door today at school. Gouged out the letters to spell 'creep.' I thought of Rod or Clay, but maybe I got other enemies I don't know about."

"Wow!" Naomi gasped. "That is so stupid. I can see Rod or Clay doing it, though. You made Rod look bad at the senior class meeting by staying nice and professional. Actually, his position was so stupid he didn't even need help. So some jerk scraped that ugly word on your car door in broad daylight. Wow. You can paint over it, right?"

"Oh, sure," Ernesto replied. "It's no problem. I got white enamel in the garage. The car looks so bad anyway. I don't mind some ugly-looking paint on the door. Who cares? Actually I've been saving up money from my pizzeria job. I'm thinking of getting a different car. Bashar gave me another raise, and I've got a nice little nest egg. I should be able to get a classier set of wheels pretty soon."

Naomi looked sad. "Oh, but the Volvo is such a safe, reliable car, Ernie," she sighed. "I hate to think of you not having it anymore. I'm kind of attached to it. In some funny way, it's like you, Ernie. Trustworthy, solid."

"Hey, thanks a lot . . . I think," her boyfriend responded. "What else am I? Boring? Not so good looking? But hey, looks aren't everything." Ernesto grinned.

Naomi gave Ernesto a friendly poke in the ribs. "I don't mean that. You're the hottest guy I ever knew, babe. Know why I like going to the beach? I love to check out your abs. Those abs are something else. But you're good and solid too, like the Volvo. You're there for anybody who needs you. When I have a problem, I don't even think twice about whether you'll help me. Like the Volvo. I don't ever wonder if the it's gonna start." Naomi giggled a little and added, "I don't know. The Volvo is sorta like a pet . . ."

"Oh man!" Ernesto groaned comically. "Now I'm stuck with a pet Volvo. If I don't find a good home for it, I'm bad. Next thing you know, you'll be naming it!"

"Viola," Naomi whispered so softly that Ernesto didn't hear her. It was the name she had given Ernesto's Volvo.

When they parked at the beach, Ernesto could smell the sharp salt air. "Babe," he announced, laughing, "prepare to see my killer abs."

CHAPTER NINE

The fall had been warm so far. The temperatures had been edging into the low nineties in the inland valleys. In the *barrio* where Cesar Chavez High School was located, it had been ninety-two during the day. Ernesto couldn't imagine a better evening for a beach barbecue.

At the beach parking lot, Ernesto stripped off his T-shirt and picked up the ice chest of soft drinks. Then the couple headed down the narrow path that led to the sand. He'd been working out, stretching, and contracting, and he was in great shape. He looked good. He liked to feel Naomi's gaze on him, a smile parting her lips.

"You *do* look fabulous, dude," Naomi announced, as she followed Ernesto down the path.

Paul Morales and Carmen Ibarra were already on the sand, getting the fire rings ready. Abel and Claudia were running late; that was unusual for them. When Paul saw Ernesto, he left his work and walked over to him. He grabbed Ernesto's hand and pumped it.

"Ernie," Paul told him, "you and your family did a world of good for Cruz and his family. You can't begin to imagine what that Sunday dinner meant to them. I was with Cruz Sunday night, and he couldn't stop talking about it. He raved about the dinner, but that wasn't the big thing."

Paul flashed his trademark smile. "The way you guys treated him and his family just blew the dude away. They felt like honored guests. The Lopez clan isn't used to that kind of attention. But you guys made them feel special. Thanks, man. You lifted that family up, and it meant the world. Be sure to tell your folks."

"Katalina really deserves the credit for it," Ernesto objected. "Andrea Lopez is her best friend, and she likes Sarah too. She just kept nagging and nagging to have the whole Lopez family over. I wasn't sure how it would all turn out, but Cruz was great."

A thought came to Ernesto's mind. "You know," he told Paul, "me and Abel were talking. Abel's gonna teach Sarah and Andrea how to make simple things like healthy salads. Poor Mr. Lopez is so busy he gives the kids junk food every day. Andrea and Sarah are pretty little girls, but they're already putting on weight. If they can just learn some basic things, Cruz and the girls can give the family a better diet."

"That would be awesome, man," Paul responded.

The last to arrive were Abel and Claudia. Paul had already stacked the burgers and hot dogs by the fire rings. It was still light,

165

but the moon was a pale beach ball hanging in the darkening sky.

As Ernesto walked over to Abel, he noticed a strange look on his friend's face. "You okay, dude?" Ernesto asked. "You look like you got something on your mind."

"Everything's cool," Abel replied, but Ernesto could see that was a lie. Abel wasn't good about hiding his feelings. Abel walked over to the fire rings to take over the grilling. From time to time, he glanced at Claudia, who was heating hot water. She looked strange too, not her usual cheerful self. Ernesto got very worried. Abel Ruiz was his best friend at Cesar Chavez High. The boys had been friends since those first few days when Ernesto arrived as a scared stranger. Ernesto didn't know what he would have done without Abel's friendship.

Abel had a lot of personal baggage. His parents—mostly his mother—always looked at him as a loser. Abel's older brother, Tomás, was the success in the family. Abel's mother loved Abel, but she always let him know that she didn't expect much of him.

Abel was a nice-looking guy, but he wasn't hot. He had a hard time getting girlfriends. He met Claudia when he started working at the doughnut shop. Much to his delight, they hit it off. Claudia attended a nearby private high school, so Abel couldn't see her during the school day. But they had a lot of fun dates, and they seemed to be a good match.

Claudia Villa was an only child. Her parents were never against her dating Abel. But they would have preferred her to be seeing a boy from the nearby private boys school. The Villas thought that Cesar Chavez was a rough place. They felt that the students there were not as nice as the private school kids.

Ernesto had taken it for granted that Abel and Claudia would be together for a long time. But now they weren't as warm and smiling with each other as they usually were. Something was clearly wrong.

Ernesto hoped it was nothing serious because the girl meant the world to Abel.

After they'd eaten their burgers, Naomi and Carmen took a walk down the beach, and Abel went to his car to get something. Claudia sat by herself staring out over the water. Ernesto edged over toward Paul as he sipped his drink.

"Paul," Ernesto said softly, "do you get the feeling Abel and Claudia are—"

"Yeah," Paul responded. "Maybe they had a fight or something."

"It'll probably blow over," Ernesto said hopefully.

Paul shrugged. "It's hard to keep a relationship going, man. I'm such a hardcore jerk; I'm amazed that Carmen puts up with me. But Carmen, she's in a class by herself. One minute, she's biting my head off about something. The next minute, she's jumping into my arms and kissing my face. She can't stay mad for more than thirty seconds. Her father looks at me like I'm a giant cockroach. Even Carmen's mom has sort of a sad look when I show up. But none of that seems to bother Carmen. I'm such a lucky fool."

Later, Ernesto took a walk down the beach with Naomi. They found a spot on the sand and spread a blanket. They sat down and listened to the rolling waves breaking on the beach. Ernesto gently pulled Naomi against him and kissed her soft lips. She snuggled against Ernesto's bare chest and whispered, "I'm crazy about you, babe. Did I ever tell you that?"

"You can never tell me often enough," Ernesto told her, "'cuz I'm even crazier about you."

They lay back on the sand and watched the pinpoint stars in the clear, dark night sky. The warm sand beneath them was cooling, and the air was getting chilly. Ernesto and Naomi pulled on sweatshirts and started to walk back to the others.

"I guess we need to make ourselves useful," Naomi remarked. "Everybody's probably breaking up stuff and packing it in. We gotta make sure the fire rings are totally cold."

"Yep," Ernesto agreed. "Hey, Naomi, before we get there, I got a question. Has Claudia said anything to you tonight?"

Naomi turned and looked at Ernesto. "About what?"

"I don't know," Ernesto shrugged, "but Abel and her don't seem as lit up as usual."

"Claudia was starting to tell me something," Naomi responded. "But then Abel came along, and she broke off. I couldn't get the drift of what she was starting to say. I think Abel's jealous of some boy at the private school."

"Abel thinks she's interested in somebody else?" Ernesto asked.

"Something like that," Naomi replied. "Claudia is kinda upset, that's for sure."

"I hope it's nothing serious, Naomi," Ernesto commented. "I really love that guy. Abel's been such a friend to me. I know how much he loves Claudia. Since they've been together, he's just come to life. She's made all the difference."

"I know," Naomi said.

The six of them packed the leftover food and drinks, bagged all the trash to take to containers, and made sure the fire rings were safe. If they were left hot, somebody stepping on them could be seriously burned.

Before he and Naomi went to the Volvo, Ernesto noticed Abel standing alone, looking out over the water. He left Naomi for a few minutes and walked over to his friend.

"Hey, man," Ernesto began, "if you need somebody to talk to, you know I'm here, don't you? Text me, call me, just come over. Anything. I'm here for you, man, okay?"

Abel turned, his dark eyes filled with pain. "Thanks, dude," he murmured.

Ernesto reached out and gave Abel a hug. "You're my *hermano*, dude. You're blood as far as I'm concerned. You always will be."

"Love you, Ernie," Abel responded in a heavy voice. Then he turned and walked over to where Claudia waited. The couple went up the path to where the cars were parked but didn't talk to each other. By the time Naomi and Ernesto reached the Volvo, they were gone.

When Ernesto got home from school on Monday, his grandparents—the Vasquezes—were in the driveway. They hadn't planned on coming for another week. But they had decided to come earlier because of *Abuela* Lena. Maria Sandoval had assured her mother that all was well and that the older woman was no burden. Yet, Eva Vasquez, her mother, felt the need to come.

Dad had come home early from school to take his mother for her doctor's appointment. Katalina and Juanita were at a neighbor's house learning to play the piano. So when Ernesto went into the house, only his mother and her parents were there.

"Hi, Grandma . . . Grandpa," Ernesto greeted.

"Hello, Ernesto," his grandmother responded. "Your mother and I are talking about finding a nice assisted living place for your father's mother. Older people are much better off with their own kind in a nice facility."

Ernesto was sure Mom was not "talking" about any such thing. He *was* sure Grandma Vasquez was trying to convince her to move *Abuela* Lena out.

"I think I'll go see little Alfredo," Mr. Vasquez said. "Even if he's sleeping, I love looking at him."

Maria Sandoval smiled at her father. "I think he's going to wake up soon," she remarked, smiling at her dad. "He loves being held. He's really a little love bug, Daddy. Go have fun."

"*Abuela* Lena loves it here," Ernesto told Eva Vasquez. "And we love having her. My sisters absolutely dote on her. She's happy here. It'd be crazy for her to move."

173

"Ernesto," Eva Vasquez objected, "don't you realize how burdened your poor mother is. Now that Lena is disabled, it's even worse. I mean, your mother has no time even for her little books now."

"As a matter of fact, Mom," Maria Sandoval interrupted, "I'm in the middle of a new book project. My agent called me last week. We talked about a science book in print and an interactive e-book. I'm really excited about it."

Ernesto did not know what his mother was talking about. He thought maybe she was making it all up to fend off her mother's attack. His mother glanced at him and smiled, "I was going to tell you all tonight at dinner, Ernie. I wanted it to be a surprise. It all came from that blue-tailed skink!"

"What?" Eva Vasquez asked, frowning.

"Yes!" Mom answered, beaming. "We're expanding on *Don't Blink, It's a Skink*. Isn't that wonderful? The blue-tailed skink will be on the cover, and we'll include all kinds of other interesting reptiles. Kids love stuff like that."

Then a serious look came to Mrs. Sandoval's face. She spoke to her mother. "Mom, I know you love me, and you're worried about me. But I'm right where I want to be, and I'm happy. I mean, isn't that what it's all about?"

"But darling," Eva Vasquez protested in a wistful voice, "you were such a bright child, such a promising young lady. The whole world was waiting for you to do wonderful things."

"And I have, Mom," Maria Sandoval insisted. "In my wildest dreams as a teenager, I never imagined I could be so happy and fulfilled as I am now. Four wonderful kids . . . a husband I love even more than when I married him . . . my books . . . my friends. I'm so lucky, Mom, there's only one thing wrong."

Eva Vasquez's eyes widened and she looked hopeful. "I knew there was something wrong. A mother knows. What is it? Tell me, darling," she demanded.

"I'm very happy and so fulfilled," Mom explained. "But my mother—whom I love very much—isn't as happy for me as she should be. If you could share my happiness, Mom, then my life would be perfect."

Eva Vasquez said nothing. Mother and daughter gazed at each other for a long second. At that moment, *Abuelo* Alfredo emerged from the bedroom, a gurgling Alfredo in his arms. "He knows me," Alfredo Vasquez announced proudly. "The minute he opened his eyes, he smiled!"

Alfredo snuggled happily in the man's arms. Alfredo Sr. commented, "His eyes, they are the same shade of blue as mine are. Do you see that? And that thick, curly hair. I had hair like that when I was a child."

"When he's older, you'll have to take him for walks, Daddy," Maria Sandoval suggested. "Just like you took me. I remember our walks as the happiest part of my childhood. When I'd get tired, you'd hoist me to your shoulders. We'd walk on, and you'd tell me the names of all the trees and flowers."

"Yes," Mr. Vasquez recalled. "I wasn't able to spend as much time with Ernesto when he was small. I was still working, but now I'm retired. We might even move down here so we're closer."

"Al!" his wife scolded. "You know we love our house in Los Angeles."

In an unusual display of courage, Mr. Vasquez said smiling, "*You* love the house, Eva. Me, not so much. What I truly love are my grandchildren. I want to get to know Katalina and Juanita better. I want to spend time with Ernesto. I want to be with little Alfredo."

Katalina and Juanita burst through the door and rushed to their grandparents. They'd seen the car in the driveway.

"*Abuela, Abuelo*," Katalina cried, hugging the Vasquezes. Eva Vasquez didn't want to be addressed as *abuela*, but the girls didn't care.

"Look," Juanita noted. "Little Alfredo loves *Abuelo*. Look how he's laughing."

"*Abuela!*" Juanita cried, grabbing Eva Vasquez's hand. "Me and Kat are learning to play the piano. Let me show you what we learned already." Juanita dragged her grandmother over to the small spinet in the corner. Eva Vasquez didn't look very pleased as the girls plunked their way through some simple tunes. But she was gracious.

Maria Sandoval and her father went into the bedroom. They put Alfredo on the bed to be changed. Little Alfredo kicked and waved his little arms as Mom cleaned him.

"You know, Maria," *Abuelo* Alfredo said softly, "your mother resented your naming your first son Ernesto, not Alfredo. She felt it was a slight. I didn't mind. I understood. Of course, Luis would want his first son named for his father. But Eva is very sensitive. She was quite upset even when you and Luis were dating."

"I know, Daddy," Maria Sandoval said quietly.

"Luis was becoming a teacher," the father went on, "and teachers don't make a lot of money. You were marrying very young and giving up the thought of college. Your mother loves you very much, Maria. She just cannot always understand that her dreams are not your dreams. The children must follow their own dreams."

"Yes, Daddy," Ernesto's mother responded. "That is how I feel about my children."

"I don't know if I can talk Eva into moving down here," Alfredo almost whispered. "If not, I'll be coming often. It's just a couple hours drive, and the train runs between Los Angeles and here. I love to ride the train. I know one thing, I'll be taking little Alfredo for many walks. I'll be getting to know Katalina and Juanita. And I'll see that wonderful boy, Ernesto, who is almost a man—and what a fine young man. It will be such a joy to me."

Little Alfredo was cleaned, diapered, and fresh. He lay comfortably in the middle of the bed. Maria Sandoval leaned her head against her father's chest and hugged him.

179

"It will be a joy for little Alfredo too," she said softly, "and for the girls and Ernesto. It broke Ernesto's heart when he was only nine and Luis's father died. They were so close. He misses his grandfather. Now he has a grandfather again."

Alfredo Vasquez tenderly kissed the top of his daughter's shining hair.

CHAPTER TEN

The seniors at Cesar Chavez High School had chosen "Estrellas fugaces" for the homecoming theme. Now they were voting for king and queen. Ernesto knew most of the girls who were candidates and a couple of the boys. At lunchtime, he went over the ballot with his friends.

"Let's see now, Mira Nuñez is running," he noted.

"She's so pretty," Naomi commented. "She did so much for the school in her sophomore and junior years. It'd be kinda nice if she got the honor."

"Yeah," Ernesto agreed, "and she had the courage to break up with Clay Aguirre. I admire her for that. When she didn't get senior class president, she was gracious about it. Not like Rod Garcia, who hates me for winning."

"Mmm, Roxie Torres is running," Carmen Ibarra remarked. "She's cute, but she's such a gossip!"

"Yvette Ozono," Ernesto announced. "Man, that would be so cool if she won. I'm gonna vote for her. She's overcome so much. She's been through the worst possible . . . losing the guy she loved to gang violence . . . the poverty."

"Yeah, you're right, and she's so nice," Naomi agreed. "She's like the top math student in the senior class. Phil Serra, her boyfriend, he's a great guy too."

"Look," Naomi pointed out, "Phil's running for king! Would it be awesome if those two won?"

"Julio Avila's running for king too," Abel Ruiz said. "He's the top guy on the track team now. You're fast, Ernie, but he's like lightning. He's brought a lot of wins to the Chavez Cougars. Old Coach Muñoz worships the dude."

"And Carlos Negrete is running," Naomi added. "He and Dom made that beautiful Chavez mural on the side of the building."

"Rod Garcia's girlfriend, Lisa Castillo, is running for queen," Carmen said, making a face. "She's rude and phony. She's kind of a witch."

"Yeah, but she's pretty," Abel objected. "Lotta guys just look at that."

"Well," Ernesto commented, "I'm going to vote for Yvette and Phil. Yvette and her family live in a crummy little apartment. I remember going over there right after Tommy Alvarado was murdered. There was her mom and a bunch of little kids, and they didn't have hardly any furniture. Yvette was a dropout from Chavez then. She was so depressed that she didn't even want to live. And look at her now."

"Ernie," Carmen said, "do you remember when Phil Serra first asked Yvette for a date? She turned him down 'cause she didn't think she was good enough for a nice guy like him? Do you remember who talked to Yvette? Who got her turned around so that accepted Phil's offer?"

Ernesto grinned. "Paul Morales. Yeah, I remember how he came on like thunder. He just about yelled in Yvette's face. He said he was a loser too, and he wasn't gonna let that get in his way. Paul really changed Yvette's life with that pep talk. Paul makes me nervous sometimes, but he's a beautiful guy."

Carmen smiled happily. She and Paul were inseparable now in spite of her parents' misgivings about him. One fateful night last year, Paul Morales had pulled into the parking lot at Hortencia's and spied Carmen in her red convertible. Carmen had received the car as a birthday gift from her parents, and it made her stand out. She was a pretty girl, but she didn't get the attention that girls like Naomi did.

Paul had yelled, "Hey, homies, check out that hot convertible." Then he added, "Whoa, check out the chick at the wheel. She's even hotter." From that moment, Carmen's life changed. No guy had ever made such a big deal of her before. Carmen fell in love with Paul Morales that very night.

Abel Ruiz looked off into the distance. He'd brought his own concoction for lunch, a salad with dressing he'd made. But he wasn't eating much. Ernesto wished he'd share what was bothering him. Surely it had something to do with Claudia, but he didn't know how bad things were.

A little later, Ernesto was walking from lunch to his afternoon classes. In the quad, he saw a group of seniors in animated conversation. Rod and Clay were in the group, along with Lisa Castillo and some of the other kids they hung with. After a few minutes, Lisa broke from the rest and began walking in the same direction as Ernesto. Ernesto had to say something to her or appear rude.

185

"Hi, Lisa," Ernesto said. "I see you're in the running for homecoming queen. Good luck. You're a pretty girl."

"Thanks," Lisa replied. "I think my real competition is Mira Nuñez. She's stunning, and she's popular too. I don't have to worry about that little twit Yvette Ozono. Everybody knows she's a gang girl. Chavez High doesn't need trash like that for homecoming queen."

Ernesto sighed deeply in disgust. "Yvette was mixed up with gangs at one time, but she's turned her life completely around. She's won the top math prize in the district. She's a really good person."

"Once a gang chick, always a gang chick," Lisa insisted. "I don't know why that poor fool Phil Serra goes with her. He's got more class than that. He could do much better than her. But I'm not worried about Yvette getting it. It's Mira who might rain on my parade."

Ernesto felt like telling Lisa off. But he kept reminding himself that he was senior class president. He couldn't speak his mind as he used to do.

Lisa continued. "Clay said he used to date Mira. He said her mom is real trashy. Lotta boyfriends. Mira wasn't as pretty when she was a junior as she is now. She was kinda fat."

Lisa laughed. "Clay said they went to the beach, and he was like embarrassed at how she looked in her bikini. I mean, Clay's always been ripped. Now Mira's lost about twenty pounds, but last summer . . ."

Lisa seemed to catch herself from saying something. She laughed again. Ernesto got the feeling that Rod and Clay were going to use dirty tricks against Mira. But he wasn't sure what those tricks might be.

The buzz around Chavez High was that Mira Nuñez and Lisa Castillo were running neck in neck in the voting. Yvette Ozono was right behind them. Mira's many activities were helping her. Lisa Castillo didn't participate in anything more than cheerleading. Ernesto wanted Yvette to win. But if she didn't, he thought Mira deserved the crown.

On Wednesday, Ernesto was coming on campus when he spotted Mira Nuñez. She was sitting on a bench and looking forlorn. Ernesto wondered whether she was having trouble at home. The last he heard, Mira's mother had a toxic boyfriend. Could he have started some real trouble? Ernesto walked over to Mira and stood there for a moment. "Mira, is there room on that bench for me?" he asked.

Mira scrunched over a little. "Sure," she said. Her eyes were red and swollen from crying. "I should just go home. I can't go to classes today."

"What's up, Mira?" Ernesto asked.

"Oh, Ernie," she whimpered. "I'm so humiliated. I just cannot believe what Clay did. I feel like I'm a crime victim!" The girl wept.

"What are you talking about, girl?" Ernesto asked.

188

Mira pulled out her iPhone. "You might as well see it, Ernie. Everybody else has. It'll be the dirty joke all over Chavez High."

Ernesto looked at the images of an overweight girl in a bikini, taken from the rear. A children's song was playing: "Piggy Wiggy, what's your name? Piggy Wiggy, what's your game?" Finally the girl turned. It was the heavier Mira Nuñez of last year.

"I didn't even know Clay took pictures of me that day last year," Mira wailed. "Why would he do such a thing? We were good then. We were dating and stuff. But he has a cruel streak. Sometimes he did stuff just to humiliate me."

Mira sobbed. "Now . . . now everybody thinks I'm fat and ugly, and they won't vote for me. They'll vote for Lisa Castillo, Rod Garcia's girlfriend. Clay did this just to please Rod. They're really tight now."

"Mira, everybody's gonna know it was a rotten, underhanded trick," Ernesto assured her. "You're a beautiful girl. Anybody can see that. Kids are gonna sympathize with you, Mira." Ernesto's mind was spinning. Deep in his heart he wanted Yvette to win, but he hated to think Mira Nuñez would lose this way.

"I don't even want to win anymore," Mira sobbed. "He's ruined it for me."

A little while later, Ernesto saw Rod walking with Lisa Castillo. They were humming the piggy song and showing images on an iPhone to two boys. The boys began laughing wildly and walked off. Ernesto waited until the boys were gone. Then he went over to Rod and Lisa. "Aren't you guys ashamed of yourself for pulling something like that?" Ernesto challenged them.

Lisa giggled, but her smile faded before Ernesto's icy scorn. "That was a purely evil and cruel stunt. The fact that you'd be part of it makes you unfit to be homecoming queen, Lisa," Ernesto told her.

"I . . . I didn't take the pictures," Lisa stammered.

"I didn't either," Rod insisted. "Mira musta posed for them. The big fat thing musta thought she looked hot."

"Mira didn't know Clay Aguirre was taking the pictures," Ernesto snarled at Rod. "He ambushed her without her knowing it."

Then he turned to Lisa. "Lisa, I hope I never want anything in my entire life so bad that I'd stoop to a stunt like this. You're trading your self-respect for a lousy homecoming queen tiara, girl. And I sincerely hope you lose." Ernesto wheeled and stomped away.

All day, Ernesto saw students at their iPhones, checking out the hilarious images everybody was talking about. He noted that the reactions were mixed. Most kids laughed, but some looked surprised. A few looked sad, and some even looked scared. Maybe, Ernesto figured, they were wondering whether anyone was taking pictures of them at a party or somewhere else. Were they thinking that humiliating pictures of them could end up online?

That night at dinner, Ernesto told his family what had happened to Mira.

"It's a whole new world out there," Luis Sandoval responded. "Our privacy can be stolen with the click of a camera. Technology is wonderful in so many ways, but it can be used to destroy people too."

"You've got to be so careful," Maria Sandoval remarked. "Don't do anything that can end up online. Don't even post things to a friend. That friend might send it somewhere else."

"I feel so bad for Mira," Ernesto sighed. "I think she would have won the homecoming thing. Now, I mean, she was so nice when she lost senior class president, and this would've been so good for her."

"You think that mean Lisa Castillo is gonna win, Ernie?" Katalina demanded. "Ernie, you gotta tell everybody what a mean, horrible person she is."

"I'd love to go around tearing her down," Ernesto responded, poking a fork at his dinner. "And I'd love to punch Clay and

Rod in the mouth and leave their teeth in the school parking lot. But I can't do stuff like that, Kat. I couldn't even do it as a student. Now that I'm senior class president, so I doubly can't do it."

"But it's not fair if she wins!" Katalina wailed. "It's like the bad guys get the reward. It's not fair!"

"Mi hija," Luis Sandoval said sadly, "it wouldn't be the first time the bad guy won."

By Thursday morning, Mrs. Sanchez, the principal, was investigating the incident. She'd announced that the responsible students could be suspended or even expelled.

But the damage was done. Mira Nuñez dropped out of the competition for homecoming queen. Her friends had tried to talk her out of her decision, but she refused to change her mind. Carmen Ibarra and Naomi Martinez had begged her to stay in the running. Everybody knew that she'd been sandbagged, they told her. That would motivate kids all the more to vote for her. They told Mira that she had done so much for the school that she deserved to win. Everybody knew that.

"You're so beautiful, Mira," Naomi told her. "You'll make a marvelous homecoming queen."

But Mira wouldn't listen. She was so deeply hurt by the gross images spread all over the school. She just couldn't take it anymore. Even if she won, she thought, people would just be thinking about the heavyset girl in the bikini.

"I'd never be able to wear a pretty dress and walk into the auditorium with a tiara on my head," Mira objected. "In my heart, I'd know most of the kids—especially the guys—they'd be thinking about that horrible fat thing on the beach. They'd just be laughing at me on the inside."

Mira could barely look at her friends, who surrounded her. "Carmen, Naomi," she explained, "I know you're trying to help me. You guys are on my side—I know that. And I appreciate it, but it's over.

It would never be fun for me. On stage, I'd hear that horrible piggy song in my head, and it would be torture for me. Just let me drop it, and get back to my normal life."

An unusually mean look entered Mira's eyes. "If Lisa Castillo wins," she snarled, "I hope the prize is ruined for her too. I hope she remembers all her life that she got it by hurting another girl. I hope the victory is sour in her mouth forever."

Lisa Castillo was elated when she heard that Mira had dropped out. Her only serious rival was gone. Now everybody thought Lisa was in.

Besides being overjoyed that Mira no longer a threat, Lisa had a secret hope. She wanted Julio Avila to be the homecoming king. He was a tall, handsome boy, and they'd look so good together walking into the auditorium. The problem was that Rod Garcia sensed what she wanted.

"If Avila does win," Rod warned Lisa, "don't freak over him, okay? Remember, we're tight. Avila's a jerk. It's okay if you walk into the auditorium with him, but you're my chick, right?"

"Sure, Rod," Lisa answered. But in her heart she wasn't sure how she felt. For a long time, she had watched the Cesar Chavez track team run. While she watched and rooted for Rod, she also noticed that Julio Avila was incredibly hot. Once, when Rod didn't run, Lisa had even flirted with Julio, but he didn't take the bait. He acted as though she was a pesky gnat that wouldn't go away.

But Lisa wasn't sure he would always feel that way. When Julio saw her in a beautiful gown, saw her lovely shoulders in the dazzling dress, he might not see her as a pesky gnat anymore. If that left Rod in her dust, Lisa didn't worry too much.

But, for now, to Rod she smiled and told a lie. "It's just that when I make that walk, I want a good-looking guy with me. What if somebody like that little dork, Phil Serra, got homecoming king? We'd both look stupid because of him."

"He'll never win," Rod Garcia insisted. "Being connected to that gang chick, Yvette Ozono, paints him with the same brush. Mosta the kids here at Chavez don't want anything to do with gangbangers like that. I mean, what would it look like if the homecoming king and queen were homies! What a black eye to the school that'd be."

Deprise Wilson was going to announce the names of the homecoming king and queen on Friday, just after classes ended.

Ernesto was in his last class with Naomi and Carmen. They all felt sick over how the election was going. Ernesto didn't like to text in class, but this time he couldn't resist. The class was supposed to be looking at a video. But Ernesto texted Naomi, "If LC wins, I'll puke."

"LOL," Naomi texted back. Naomi believed more strongly in the Chavez students than Ernesto did. She didn't believe that Lisa could win after that dirty trick on Mira.

197

"If LC wins, I won't even come to homecoming," Carmen texted. She shared Ernesto's grim fears.

Finally, the class ended, and there was dead silence, as everyone waited for the announcement. Ernesto gripped the edge of his desk until his fingers ached. Then Ms. Wilson's bubbly voice came over the PA system.

"This is so amazing!" Deprise Wilson burbled. "This is going to be the best homecoming week ever in the history of Cesar Chavez High School. On behalf of all the senior teachers and the wonderful seniors in the class, I want to congratulate the king and queen of homecoming: Phil Serra and Yvette Ozono!"

Ernesto leaped from his seat and grabbed Naomi and Carmen, hugging them both. The three of them danced around the room. They could hear cheers exploding from other classrooms too.

As the cheering died down, the students collected their books and things to leave. All Ernesto could think of was that dark day when he and his father were among the few mourners at the funeral of Tommy Alvarado. Tommy was the boy Yvette had loved. He'd died because he loved a girl who had dared to break out of the clutches of a brutal gang. Ernesto didn't know Tommy Alvarado well. He was a student in Luis Sandoval's class, and Dad said he was a fine young man. Ernesto's lips barely moved and nobody heard him say, "Tommy, this one's for you."

Ernesto and Naomi were quiet as they walked to the parking lot. Ernesto didn't know what his girl was thinking about; he had his own thoughts. He was sorting out the winners and losers in his life.

Clay, Lisa, Rod—they proved themselves to be losers. Not because Clay lost Naomi to Ernesto. Not because Lisa didn't become homecoming queen. Not because Rod lost the election. They were losers because winning was more important to them than anything—or anyone—else. They valued all the wrong things.

Ernesto felt grateful for all the winners he could count as friends. Cruz and Beto could have been hard core gangbangers, but they were studying the building trades. Dom and Carlos were seniors, not aimless taggers on the street. Yvette was a topnotch math student, not a dropout. Naomi and Abel and all the other kids involved in the freshmen program—they were all winners. Their hearts and minds were in the right place. And, despite the loss of their mom and wife, the Lopezes were working hard to carry on, day after day. Maybe they were the biggest winners of all.

"I'm in good company," Ernesto reflected and smiled. "I'm in the company of winners."